“I’ve been think

“We’re both adults.
other quickly, in a p
due to circumstances beyond our control. But no matter how unusual those circumstances may have been, they don’t change the fact that we’re in this situation now.”

“And…what exactly is our situation?”

She took a deep breath. “I’ve been thinking a lot about that moment in quarantine.”

Jack waited without breathing. He thought his heart might have stopped.

She went on. “You know the moment I mean. When we…kissed.” Her eyes flickered straight to his, and he knew his heart hadn’t stopped after all. It was pounding jackhammer-hard.

“I don’t know about you,” she said, “but I’ve had a hard time not thinking about it. The kiss, I mean. And I know that you said you don’t believe in relationships. Well, neither do I. But in a way, that makes us kind of ideal for one another right now.”

“How so?” he said.

“Well,” she continued, looking nervous, “anything involving emotions would probably be a terrible idea—for both of us. But then I started thinking that not every relationship has to involve emotions. Some relationships have a more…physical…basis.”

Dear Reader,

Aloha and mahalo for reading *From Hawaii to Forever*.

Hawaii is one of the most special places I've been fortunate enough to visit. There's something about the palm trees, the mountains and the sound of the ocean that is instantly relaxing.

But relaxing doesn't come easily to Dr. Kat Murphy. When she arrives in Hawaii, she's at a low point. She's been jilted, she's lost her job and nothing in her life is turning out the way she thought it would. Worst of all, after spending years working to get to the top of her field, Kat realizes that she's completely forgotten how to relax and live in the moment.

Fortunately, she meets Jack, a daring paramedic with a painful past. Jack suggests that Kat doesn't need peace and quiet to relax—she needs excitement and fun. Kat takes one look at Jack and decides that he's right… and that he's just the one to provide the thrills she's looking for.

I hope you have as much fun reading about Kat and Jack's journey as I did writing about it. And feel welcome to stop by my website, juliedanvers.wordpress.com, or say hello on Twitter, @_juliedanvers.

Warmly,

Julie Danvers

FROM HAWAII TO FOREVER

—

JULIE DANVERS

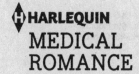

HARLEQUIN
MEDICAL
ROMANCE

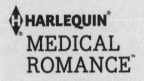

HARLEQUIN®
MEDICAL
ROMANCE™

Recycling programs
for this product may
not exist in your area.

ISBN-13: 978-1-335-14946-6

From Hawaii to Forever

Copyright © 2020 by Alexis Silas

Harlequin Enterprises ULC
22 Adelaide St. West, 40th Floor
Toronto, Ontario M5H 4E3, Canada
www.Harlequin.com

Printed in U.S.A.

To my mother, my first and best copy editor.

CHAPTER ONE

As SHE STEPPED off the plane in Honolulu, Dr. Katherine Murphy shook the last few drops of water from her snow boots. When she'd boarded the plane in Chicago, snow had caked her boots and dusted her winter coat. A few droplets of water were all that had managed to survive the flight, and now she shook them off with relish. Back home, temperatures were below freezing and the snow was several inches deep. But here in Hawaii a steady, gentle breeze rustled through the palm trees.

Goodbye, ice and cold, Kat thought, stepping into the early-morning sun.

Although she was still wearing the winter clothes she'd had on when she left, her carry-on luggage contained sixteen bathing suits, a floppy hat and sunglasses, and numerous pairs of flip-flops. At the last minute she'd remembered to throw in her white coat and a stethoscope before zipping the small suitcase shut.

The rest of her belongings had already been shipped separately to her new home on the island of Oahu.

Kat couldn't believe that just three weeks ago, she had been one of the most respected physicians in Chicago. Three weeks ago she'd expected to be promoted to head of the internal medicine department at Chicago Grace Memorial, the prestigious hospital where she'd completed her residency and spent most of her career. Three weeks ago her future had seemed stable, secure and predictable.

Three weeks ago she and Christopher had been days away from getting married.

Kat glanced at the faint line on her finger where her engagement ring used to be. She still felt a hard lump rise in her throat every time she thought about the breakup.

Tears blurred her eyes, but she fought them back and tried to smile as an airport attendant greeted her warmly and placed a beautiful *lei* of purple orchids over her head. Kat shook the tears away and raised her chin. Her new job as an internist and infectious disease specialist at Oahu General Hospital was a chance for a fresh start, and there was no point in dwelling on the past.

Goodbye, old life, she thought. *And goodbye, Christopher.*

Leaving her steady, predictable life in Chicago and moving to Hawaii ranked very high on the list of things Kat had thought she would never do. But then, she'd also never thought she would lose her promotion, her job and her fiancé on the same day.

In her mind, she thought of it as the Day of Doom.

Three weeks ago she'd huddled under a thick down blanket inside her apartment, the outside world covered with an even thicker layer of February snow, trying to figure out how she could ever face the world again. Everything she'd ever worked for—her medical career, her wedding, her family's hopes and dreams for her—had disappeared in an instant.

She'd just begun thinking about how long she could reasonably hide in her apartment before she would need to forage for food when her best friend from medical school had called with an intriguing proposal. Selena was the clinical director at a small hospital in Hawaii, and she'd called to ask if Kat knew anyone who would be interested in working in Honolulu for one year, to assist with research into and treatment of a rare strain of flu.

Kat had shocked herself by volunteering for the position.

Her mother and her friends in Chicago had

been equally shocked. Kat couldn't blame them. Making spontaneous, impulsive decisions wasn't exactly her strongest personality trait. From the time she was sixteen and had decided she wanted to be a doctor, every important decision she'd made had been the result of careful planning and research. Everything in her life from her career to her closest relationships had been built on a foundation of logical, practical choices.

Kat's friends told her she was "certifiably Type A," and Kat had to admit that they were right. She was never one to leap without looking first.

But that had been the old Kat. The Kat who had been blissfully unaware of how much life could change in a single day.

Kat had always thought that her cautious, well-planned approach to life would protect her from unexpected surprises. She'd believed that if she was prepared for anything then she would be able to handle whatever life threw at her. But now, as she felt the empty space on her ring finger, she realized that what people said about best-laid plans was true: you could plan and plan, but you never really knew what would happen next.

Kat had spent her life planning, but she still hadn't been prepared for the breakup. And she definitely hadn't been prepared to lose her job—a job she'd loved and had spent her entire career working toward.

Yes, m'dear, you have definitely hit a low point, Kat thought to herself as she stepped out of the airport.

And caught her breath.

She had never seen such lush natural beauty in her life. Pink and yellow plumeria flowers lined the sidewalk, their scent wafting toward her and mixing with the perfume arising from the *lei* of orchids she wore around her neck. In the distance, mountains rose to meet a cloudless blue sky. Each path was framed by tall palm trees with large fronds that waved gently in the cool breeze.

Kat stopped and took in a slow, deep breath. The air itself smelled of flowers, and she wanted to savor the scent.

As she inhaled, she suddenly wondered when she had last stopped to breathe so deeply. She couldn't remember. Her life after medical school had been all about the fast pace of the ER. Someone had always needed her time or her attention, and needed it right away. But now, for the first time in years, there was no emergency to attend to. In this moment no one was expecting anything from her. No life-or-death decisions awaited her attention.

In this moment, all she had to do was breathe.

She blinked in amazement at herself. Thirty seconds in Hawaii and she was already stopping to smell the roses—or, in this case, the hibiscus. It was a decidedly un-Kat-like thing to do, and yet she felt more like herself than she had in weeks.

After everything that had happened she'd begun to feel as though she didn't even know who she was anymore. But now, as she gazed at the fairyland-like landscape before her, she started to feel something she hadn't felt in several weeks—something she hadn't even realized she'd lost after the Day of Doom.

It was hope.

Hope and something more than that—excitement.

There was something about the mountains in the distance that suggested endless possibilities, and Kat closed her eyes and noticed that the gentle rushing sound in the background wasn't just the wind; the ocean was adding its voice to the air as well. She was well on her way to falling in love at first sight—with Hawaii.

Maybe I'm not at such a low point after all, she thought. *Maybe this is the start of something.*

As she gazed at the natural beauty around her Kat realized that she didn't want to go straight to her new apartment. Going directly to her new home and getting things settled was something the old Kat would do. The old Kat would want to carefully organize her things and research her new neighborhood for essentials like the grocery store and the post office. But the new Kat, she decided, was going to have different priorities. And the new Kat's first order of business was to relax.

But how?

It had been so long since she'd had a moment to herself that she had absolutely no idea what relaxing even meant to her. In all her years of study, after all her classes on chemistry and human anatomy and physiology, she had overlooked one important thing. She had forgotten to learn how to relax.

She resisted the urge to look up a dictionary definition of the word *"relax"* on her phone.

I guess this is what comes of all work and no play, she thought.

She hoped she hadn't completely lost her ability to live in the moment. She had dreamed of becoming a doctor at an early age, and it had been a dream that required an incredible amount of study and discipline. She'd been so focused on her medical career that she'd never had the chance to have a wild, carefree adolescence.

Well, maybe it was time. Could someone in

their late twenties still have a wild adolescence? Kat decided she would damn well try.

This year in Hawaii would be her chance to learn how to let loose and be spontaneous. She'd spent her entire life being responsible, and where had it gotten her? Jobless. Jilted—practically at the altar. If all her careful planning, her endless pro-con lists and her thoughtful decision-making had led to so much heartbreak, then maybe it was time to try a different approach to life.

She only had one year. One year away from the expectations and preconceptions of everyone who knew her. Surely there was no better place to learn how to relax and live in the moment than a gorgeous setting such as this?

She heard the faint sound of the ocean again and it deepened her resolve. This year wasn't just going to be about putting Christopher behind her, she decided. It would be about putting the old Kat behind her.

But how did one *learn* to relax?

It can't be that hard, she thought. *If I can master organic chemistry, I can master this.*

In fact, Kat decided, she might be able to approach learning how to relax and getting over Christopher in much the same way she had gotten through organic chemistry and her other difficult classes. She would make a detailed list of her goals and then follow through with each step.

A small voice in the back of her head suggested that this might be the most Type A way that she could possibly approach relaxation, but she chose to ignore it.

How to relax in an island paradise while getting over a devastating breakup. Step one: find a beach, she thought.

Kat looked down at her snow boots in dismay. Considering the cold in Chicago, and on the flight, the boots had been a sensible choice. But now that she was here they looked ridiculous. Her feet were stifled; she couldn't wait to feel sand beneath her toes.

She had her favorite blue-and-yellow-striped bikini on underneath her heavy winter clothes. She'd fantasized about going for a swim on her first day here in Hawaii, but she'd thought she'd see her new home first. Now that she was actually here, it seemed impossible to wait.

A few moments of research on her phone informed her that the nearest beach was "a pleasant twenty-minute walk from the airport." Surely there would be somewhere she could change out of her clothes?

Kat hitched her carry-on bag over her shoulder and headed toward the water, her face set with determination. She was going to learn how to relax or die trying.

Jack Harper wasn't usually an early riser, but he'd been wandering the beach since dawn. He held his father's letter crumpled in his fist. Choice lines were burned into his brain.

> *Many medical schools have a rolling admissions policy.*
> *I could make a few phone calls and you could easily start in the winter semester.*

Jack ran his hand through his dark hair in frustration. He *liked* being a paramedic, dammit. But it didn't matter how many times he'd told his father he was never going back to medical school. There was no other path that his parents could understand.

> *It's time to apply yourself.*
> *You've had your fun in Hawaii. But now it's time to come back to real life.*

To his father, real life meant Lincoln, Nebraska.

Jack couldn't imagine a place more different from Hawaii.

Lincoln was as fine a hometown as any, but he'd been glad when he was able to exchange the cornfields, cows and cold winters of his childhood for the lush mountain landscape surrounding Honolulu.

His parents, grandfather, and two brothers still lived in Lincoln, where they were all physicians. Both of his parents were highly respected, world-renowned medical researchers, his younger brother Todd had joined their grandfather's small family practice, and his older brother Matt was a surgeon.

Five doctors in the family. Five Type A personalities who were convinced that they were always right. Five people with egos larger than the Hawaiian mountains that loomed over the ocean.

In Jack's opinion, five doctors in the family was plenty. Three years of medical school had been enough to convince him that a doctor's life wasn't for him. He was much happier as a paramedic—especially here on the island of Oahu.

After dropping out of medical school to join the Navy SEALS—another life decision his parents had disapproved of—he'd completed his basic training in Hawaii and never lived anywhere that felt more like home. He'd rescue a burn victim one day and deliver a baby the next—all while surrounded by an island paradise that meant more to him than anywhere else on earth.

He loved his job—both for the adrenaline rush and for the opportunities it gave him to save lives. But his parents wouldn't take his career choices or his desire to live in Hawaii seriously, and they continued to act as though he were on some sort of extended vacation.

He and his parents were very different people.

Nowhere was this more evident than in the last paragraph of his father's letter.

> *You're thirty-one years old. You have to start thinking about your future.*
> *Plenty of women in Nebraska would like to start a family, and your mother's getting older and would like more grandchildren—*

At that point Jack had stopped reading. He couldn't believe either of his parents would bring up marriage after his older brother Matt's betrayal. Matt—the golden boy of the family.

Jack snorted. It had been four years since he'd spoken with Matt or Sophie, but Jack's heart still twinged every time he thought about his older brother and his former fiancée. After being betrayed by the two most important people in his life, the last thing he wanted was to get emotionally involved in a relationship again.

As far as Jack was concerned, getting emotionally attached meant getting hurt, and that wasn't something he was willing to put himself through again. Oh, he'd had his share of dates, and there were many women willing to enjoy his company for an evening, or even a few evenings. There were certainly plenty of tourists who seemed to want Jack to fulfill their fantasies of an exotic island fling while on vacation, and Jack was happy to oblige.

But he was careful never to get too involved with anyone. If protecting his heart meant that he had to keep his guard up and keep his distance, then so be it.

Jack smoothed out the letter one last time, then crumpled it into his fist again. He resisted the urge to throw it into the ocean. The sky was clear, the water was calm and perfect, and there was no point in brooding on the beach about a past he couldn't change. He and Sophie were done, and had been for a long time. Everything that had passed between him and Matt and Sophie was long in the past.

So why did all of it still bother him so much?

Sometimes Jack wondered if keeping himself emotionally distant from everyone had actually made it harder to recover from his disastrous engagement to Sophie. But when he thought about the memories it was too painful. He hadn't just lost Sophie—he'd lost his brother, too. The one person he'd thought he could count on, no matter what.

Growing up in a family full of doctors had had its own unique pressures. Sometimes it felt to Jack as though he'd begun to feel the weight of his family's expectations the moment he was born. But, as much as Jack had felt pressured to succeed at school and in his career, it was nothing compared to what Matt had gone through.

Matt, two years older than Jack, had experienced all the pressure Jack had as well as the added expectations that had gone along with being the oldest Harper sibling. Their parents had always expected Matt to be responsible for Jack, and as a child Matt had taken that responsibility seriously. Whenever Jack had been hurt, whenever he'd had trouble with friends or begun struggling in school, he'd been able to talk to Matt about it.

In return, Jack had hero-worshipped Matt throughout their childhood. If Jack was honest with himself, he'd hero-worshipped Matt for a good part of his adulthood, too.

He'd always thought that he and Matt would stand by each other, no matter what. But after Matt had confessed what had happened with Sophie, Jack hadn't been able to stand being in the same room with him. They hadn't spoken in four years.

A faint cry for help broke through his thoughts and he scanned the water with the trained eyes of a first responder. There—a woman swimming, far out from the shore. Too far. And going farther. She was caught in a rip current that was carrying her out into the ocean, and she was going to exhaust herself trying to swim against it.

Jack snapped into action. This was one of the quieter beaches; there were no lifeguards on duty. He dialed the emergency number on his phone and let the dispatch unit know what he was about to do. Then he dropped his phone and stripped off his shirt, revealing a smooth, well-muscled chest and the powerful arms of a former Navy SEAL.

A crowd of children who had been playing in the surf began to gather on the beach, having spotted the danger the woman was in.

"Let me borrow that," he said to one of the children, grabbing the boy's body board without waiting for a response.

He ran out into the ocean, letting the rip current do the work of carrying him out to the swimmer. When he finally reached her, he could see he'd been right. She'd been trying to fight the current instead of swimming parallel to the shore. And she was clearly terrified. He knew he could get them both back to safety, but first he'd need to calm her down.

Despite the woman's terror, he couldn't help but notice her fiery red hair. He'd always liked redheads...

Focus, he thought. *She has to stay calm. Help her relax.*

"Looks like you swam out a little further than you planned," Jack teased, attempting to lighten her fear. "You do realize it's not possible to swim all the way back to the mainland, right? You'll need to book a flight for that."

The woman coughed and choked. She looked frightened, but Jack could tell she was doing the best she could to keep her fear from overwhelming her. He admired that. Most of the time during water rescues the bulk of his work involved keeping the victim from making things worse by panicking. But this woman was doing her best to follow his instructions.

"The current..." she gasped. "It's too strong. We'll never get back to shore."

Jack forced himself to stay calm, even as the rip current continued to pull both of them further from the shore.

"Of course we'll get back," he said. "But first, I need you to relax."

He put as much warmth and confidence into his voice as he could, but for some reason, at the word *"relax"* the woman's eyes seemed to widen in terror—as though Jack had told her she'd need to survive by learning how to fly, or something equally impossible.

He decided to see if he could get his arms around her—the sooner she stopped fighting the current, the better.

"I'm going to put my arm under your shoulders, okay?" he said.

He swam behind her and slipped a firm arm under her shoulders. The support he lent her had the desired effect: once her body was directly against his she stopped struggling against the water and allowed his strength to keep her afloat.

"Can you hold on to this?"

He put the body board he'd borrowed in front of her, and she clutched at it.

"Good," he said approvingly. Her panic seemed to be receding by the minute. He had to admire how quickly she was gaining control of herself; most people would still be struggling and swallowing seawater at this point.

"What's your name?" he asked her.

"Kat," she said, with a strangled gasp.

Good, Jack thought. If she could speak, then her airways were still clear.

"Kat, I need you to listen to me," he said. "We're going to survive this, but you have to trust me. If you do everything I say I promise you that we're going to get to shore. But the first thing I need you to do is stay calm."

"I'll try," she said.

He chuckled. "I can feel you trembling." She scowled at him, and he quickly added, "It's all right to be scared, but you don't need to be— because we're going to get out of this. First time getting caught in a rip current?"

She nodded. "It's my first time swimming in the ocean. First day in Hawaii, actually."

He could see that she was trying to talk herself into a calmer state, and was doing her best to keep a cool head. She had nerves of steel. He also couldn't help but notice the lithe shape of her body as she clung to him.

First things first, he told himself sternly. Maybe they should get back on dry land before he started trying to find out anything more about her. Most likely she was one of the thousands of tourists who came each month, eager for adventure and completely unprepared for the dangers of the ocean.

"Well, *aloha* and welcome to Oahu, Kat. Can you lean forward onto this body board? If you rest on your arms, I can paddle us in. Don't worry, I won't let you go."

* * *

Somehow Kat knew that he was telling her the truth.

At first, amidst her terror and the waves going over her head, it had been hard for her to get a good look at this man who had swum out to help her. All she'd been able to sense was a well-muscled, masculine presence and a steady, reassuring voice. A voice that was warm and soothing, like a spoonful of honey.

But he'd reached her with surprising speed, and she tried to trust that he knew what he was doing.

Pressing her between himself and the flotation device he had with him, he used his body to help her gain leverage as she shifted herself onto the board. As soon as she was resting entirely on it, he let go of her waist to swim beside her, and she felt a twinge of regret as the supportive arms released her.

"Great job," he said. "Hard part's over. Now just keep holding on while I tow you in. We'll be back to shore before you know it."

He continued swimming by her side, guiding the board as he pulled them both parallel to the shore. A rough wave knocked them unexpectedly, and Kat felt a sharp pain in her leg. She must have let out a yelp because the man instantly grabbed her around the waist again.

"What is it?" he said, his face concerned.

"My leg," she said. "I must have scraped it against something. I don't think it's bad."

"Just hang in there," he said. "We're almost back to the beach."

To Kat's relief, the shore was becoming closer and closer, until finally she felt the ocean waves pushing them both toward the beach instead of pulling them away.

She collapsed in a heap on the sand and he fell beside her, one arm draped protectively over her body. They both lay there for a moment, exhausted. He was close enough that Kat could feel the heat radiating from his body next to her on the shore.

She turned to thank her rescuer.

She'd been grateful for his strength during the rescue, but now that she was back on dry land she was able to appreciate quite a bit more than just his strength.

His eyes were the exact same shade as the Hawaiian ocean—a blue-green-turquoise. He was muscular, but his physique was track-star-slim. A shock of dark hair fell over his forehead, and Kat had to resist a sudden urge to run her fingers through it. Their eyes locked, and for a moment Kat felt an electric charge between them.

His arm still rested over her. Sheltering her. He was gazing down at her, making sure she was all right. She tried to speak, but it came out as a cough, and it was several moments before she was able to recover.

"That's it," he said. "You've had a nasty shock. Take some time to let yourself breathe."

She sat up. He pulled his arm away and leaned back from her. Was it wishful thinking, or did he seem to move his arm slowly, as though he wasn't ready to let go of her?

As Kat lay on the beach, slowly regaining her breath, she gradually became aware of her bedraggled appearance. She was covered in muddy sand and the water that she'd coughed up, and her hair hung in strings around her face. But she was alive—thanks to the man next to her, whoever he was. His eyes radiated concern, and he patted her back gently as they both waited for her airway to clear fully.

"I'm all right," she told him, as soon as she was breathing steadily. "All this attention is unnecessary, really. But I do have to thank you for saving my life, Mr.—?"

"Jack Harper," he said.

"Well, Mr. Harper, thank you," she said.

"Don't mention it," he said. "Just give your body the time it needs to recover."

Kat sat with her knees bent and her feet flat against the sand. She held her head down, trying to slow her breathing. Keeping her head down also had the added effect of distracting her from the fact that Jack Harper was still sitting quite close to her, his powerfully built body radiating heat, his eyes examining her face with concern.

"I don't know how you can be so casual," she said. "I was certain we were both going to die."

"It was dangerous, but you kept calm and that was half the battle," he said.

She shuddered, thinking of how close she'd come to being swept out into the ocean. "Maybe I looked calm, but I definitely didn't feel it. I always thought I was a strong swimmer, but I wasn't prepared for those currents. I was trying to swim parallel to the shore, but it seemed like no matter what direction I went in the current wanted to pull me somewhere else."

"You aren't the first person to be surprised by the strength of a Hawaiian rip current. It's a shame that your first swim here nearly killed you—especially on your first day. That's no way to welcome you to the islands."

"Really? And here I was hoping that almost drowning on my first day here would turn out to be some sort of tradition." She laughed. And then, before she could stop herself, she said, "Maybe a better way to celebrate arriving in Hawaii and surviving a near-death experience would be to take my rescuer out for dinner sometime."

She couldn't believe she'd said that. She wasn't anywhere near ready to date again. But she wouldn't mind hearing that rich, deep voice more often. Or feeling those arms around her again. Preferably in a situation where she wasn't about to drown.

Learning to relax. Step two, her brain piped up. *Find an island hottie to help you move on from your devastating breakup.*

Stop it, she told herself.

She'd just been jilted at the altar—well, technically there had still been three days until the wedding, but it had been close enough that she felt jilted. The last thing she needed was to get involved with anyone right now. She needed to get her mind off Jack's voice and arms right away. What was she *thinking*, offering to buy him dinner?

Kat forced herself to shift her attention away from Jack's beach-tanned body. This was no time for distractions, she told herself firmly. She'd just come close to getting swept out to sea, and she was still shaken by the thought of what might have happened if Jack hadn't been there to help her back to shore. She needed to clear her head and get her bearings. She also needed to find a way to turn her attention from Jack Harper's taut skin and chiseled chest muscles so she could focus on what he was saying.

"I appreciate the offer, but there's no need to thank me," said Jack. "It's part of the job." He motioned to where an ambulance had arrived, further down the beach.

"Are you a doctor?" she asked.

"Paramedic," he replied. "And I'm sorry to say that any dinner plans will have to wait—because before you do anything else we need to get you to a hospital to get checked out. We're not far from Oahu General Hospital—I'll go with you."

"Oahu General? Oh, no. I can't go there."

Now that Kat no longer feared for her life, she was becoming deeply embarrassed about the commotion her rescue had caused. More than anything, she wanted to avoid being taken to a hospital—especially Oahu General.

She could think of few things more humiliating than showing up to her new hospital as a patient, wearing nothing but a bikini. And she definitely didn't think it would be a good idea to spend more time in close quarters with Jack. If she wasn't careful that voice and those eyes would start to have an effect on her. And she had no intention of diving headlong into a fling with the first man she met in Hawaii—no matter how closely his eyes matched the color of the ocean.

"Really, I'm fine," she said.

"You're bleeding," he told her.

"What?" Kat looked down at her leg, surprised. The place where she'd felt that pain in her leg while Jack was towing her to shore had a gash of about an inch that was trickling blood. "Oh, crap. That must have happened when I hurt my leg, back in the water. It doesn't look serious to me, though."

Privately, she thought that she might need a few stitches, but she wasn't about to let Jack know that.

As he leaned in closer she caught his scent: a masculine blend of sunblock, salt water and sand. He smelled like the ocean, like the hint of salt in the air that had filled her with such excitement and called her to the beach the moment she'd stepped off the plane. She definitely needed to stay as far away from him as possible if she wanted to avoid making a fool of herself.

"It doesn't even hurt that much," she said, though she was gritting her teeth through the stinging pain that was now beginning to make itself felt.

"I'm sure it doesn't, but that's the point," said Jack. "You've just had a near-death experience, and adrenaline is coursing through your system. Right now you probably feel like you can do anything—but that's just the adrenaline. It can mask a lot of problems, including pain. You might think you're fine, but humor me—it's best for you to get to the hospital so we can get you stitched up."

"There's really no need," said Kat briskly.

But she could see that Jack wasn't going to give up easily, so she decided to try appealing to him as a medical professional.

"Look, to tell you the truth I'm a doctor, and I can take care of this myself. I'm starting my first day working at Oahu General on Monday, and I really don't want their first impression of me to be...*this*." Kat motioned to her string bikini.

Was it her imagination, or had his expression seemed to change when she'd revealed she was a doctor? For a split second it had seemed as though a shadow had passed over his face. Most people seemed to be *more* at ease with her when she revealed her profession, but if anything Jack almost seemed...disappointed?

But then he sighed and said, "Doctors always make the worst patients."

Oh. He had a valid point. As a doctor, she'd always had a difficult time allowing herself to be in the patient role, and she knew many colleagues who felt the same way. It was hard to sit back and let someone else follow procedure when she could feel her own natural tendency to take charge of the situation rising within her. Also, she hated being the center of attention.

As she took in Jack's piercing blue eyes she knew she shouldn't want to be the center of *his* attention. Her knees were still shaking, and she had a feeling that it wasn't just the onset of hypothermia.

She hoped he wouldn't notice. But of course he did. He was clearly a skilled paramedic, and Kat suspected that he didn't miss much.

"Your knees are shaking," he said. "You should know better than anyone that the biggest risk after a near-drowning in water of any temperature is hypothermia. You shouldn't be going anywhere until we can make sure your core body temperature hasn't dropped too low."

Kat groaned inwardly. Her irritation was all the worse because she knew that Jack was right. She shouldn't take care of the cut on her leg by herself—especially with the risk of hypothermia. His stubbornness was a wall she wouldn't get past, and he clearly wasn't going to be intimidated by her medical credentials.

She couldn't decide whether his determination to take care of her was incredibly annoying or attractive. A little of both, she thought.

And it didn't help that the small, rebellious voice in the back of her mind was wholly in agreement with Jack, and was shouting that spending some time in the close quarters of an ambulance with him wouldn't be an entirely unwelcome experience.

Just get in! the voice screamed. *He can be your next impulsive decision!*

Enough of that, she told herself.

Jack Harper was certainly attractive; there was no question of that. Those blue-green eyes of his seemed to change shade every minute, as though their color changed with his mood.

But Kat had felt herself getting swept away by the ocean, just moments ago. That had been scary enough. The last thing she needed now was to let herself get swept away by someone she'd just met.

Although she had to admit that Jack's air of authority was rather refreshing. She could see that no matter how much she argued he was taking her to the hospital—even if she went kicking and screaming.

As a respected internal medicine physician, Kat wasn't used to having anyone disagree with her. Her decisions were almost never questioned by her team. To have someone insist on taking care of *her* for once, in spite of all her protestations, was an utterly new experience.

It was almost a little bit sexy.

But sexy was the last thing Kat was looking for.

Not now.

Not three weeks after Christopher. Not after the disaster of their almost-wedding.

"Is it really necessary?" she asked, knowing her appeal was doomed.

"You know it is," he said.

His voice was that of a determined man who would not be denied.

Definitely a little bit sexy, the rebellious voice in her head noted.

She didn't want this kind of complication right now. She didn't want to be attracted to anyone. Three weeks ago she hadn't thought she was even capable of feeling interested in anyone else, because she'd been about to marry the love of her life. She should be returning from her honeymoon now—not standing on a tropical beach arguing with a frustratingly attractive paramedic who didn't understand when to quit.

Kat saw the stubborn set of Jack's jaw and realized that she really was going to arrive at her new place of work borderline hypothermic, muddy, and wearing a string bikini—in the company of one of the most attractive men she'd ever seen.

This, she thought, was the opposite of learning how to relax.

CHAPTER TWO

KAT DECIDED THAT if there was no chance of changing Jack's mind, she would try bargaining with him instead.

"I'll go if you insist, but at least let me find something different to wear," she said.

Riding in an ambulance with Jack while wearing nothing but a bikini would be bad enough, but she would do anything to prevent her new co-workers from forming their first impression of her while she was nearly naked and dripping wet.

"Do you have anything else with you that you could put on?" Jack asked.

"Oh!" Kat remembered. "My luggage. It's right over there, down the beach."

She started to rise, but Jack pushed her down firmly. He wrapped a blanket around her and tucked in the ends as though she were a child. Kat's cheeks burned.

She started to protest, but Jack stopped her.

"I'm not taking any risks just because you're a doctor who thinks she knows better than a paramedic. Sit still and I'll bring your luggage to you."

He headed down the beach while Kat fumed. As much as she didn't want to admit it, she was secretly glad that Jack had pushed her back into a sitting position. Her legs felt like jelly, and it would have been difficult to stand. And it was nice to have the blanket. But she needed him to understand that, as a doctor, she was perfectly capable of deciding what she did or did not need for herself.

When he returned with her things she said, "Look, this is very kind of you, but all this attention just isn't necessary. I happen to be an excellent doctor. I was the youngest chief resident of internal medicine that Chicago Grace Memorial Hospital ever had."

He rolled his eyes. "I'm sure you were."

"And I graduated from Northwestern University in just three years. I was in the top five of my class at medical school."

"Sounds like you're very smart."

Now her cheeks were burning with a different kind of embarrassment. Would he think she was the kind of person who bragged about her achievements? She realized that she was doing exactly that. Why was she acting this way? It was more than just wanting to appear competent in front of a potential new colleague. For some reason she couldn't explain, she wanted Jack to think well of her.

"I'm just trying to say that you don't need to fuss over me. You don't need to treat me like a patient," she said.

"Because doctors always know best, right?" he replied.

She was flustered. "Well…yes. Frankly, I have the most medical expertise between the two of us. I think I'm qualified to decide whether or not I'm all right."

He looked directly into her eyes and she felt a jolt go through her. His gaze was really quite arresting.

"As far as I'm concerned you are *my* patient," he said. "No matter what your medical background is, I'm the one responsible for taking care of you right now, and I intend to see that responsibility through."

His voice was firm, but warm and resonant, and she felt all her resistance melt into a puddle under his gaze. She could listen to that voice all day… She made another feeble attempt to protest, but her breath caught in her throat as he continued.

"You may think you're all right but, as I said before, that's the adrenaline pushing you through. You swallowed a lot of water out there, and I'm not leaving you alone until I'm sure you're stable."

The point apparently settled, he lifted her luggage onto the back of the ambulance and began to rummage through it.

"Hey!" she cried. "That's my stuff! How about a little privacy?" What did he think he was doing, rummaging through her personal things?

"Here we go," he said, pulling her white coat out from beneath a tangle of bathing suits and flip-flops. "Looks like your sweater's all sandy—you don't want to put that back on. But you can wear this."

She pulled the white coat over her swimsuit and wrapped it around herself. "Are you always this stubborn and bossy?" she said.

"Afraid so," he replied. "Especially where my patients are concerned—no matter where they ranked in their class at medical school."

As irritating as he was, Kat had to admire his persistence. Jack Harper might have his flaws, but being lax about patient care obviously wasn't one of them. His stubbornness both annoyed and intrigued her. Who *was* this commandeering man with the arms that had fit so perfectly around her waist?

At least she had one clue: the tattoo in flow-ing script along his arm. "'The only easy day was yesterday,'" she read. "You were a Navy SEAL?"

He nodded, clearly surprised. "Most people don't recognize the motto," he said.

"My grandfather was a SEAL," she said. "He always said Navy guys make the best boyfriends."

She flushed even more deeply. Why had she said a thing like that? She sounded like some sort of man-hungry flirt. It was all *his* fault—he had some sort of effect on her that made her want to punch him and jump into his arms all at once.

Her resolve to get away from him before she embarrassed herself further returned. She removed the blanket and tucked her white coat around herself. "Look, it's very kind of you to offer me an ambulance ride, but I'll be fine on my own," she said.

"Be my guest," he said, clearly deciding on a different tack. "But, just so you know, it's a long walk, and I'm going to be driving alongside you the whole way."

"That's your prerogative," she said.

She stood up, prepared to march away from the beach—and immediately began to sink into the sand as her legs shook under her. Her entire body was shaking.

Just before she fell onto the sand Jack caught her and lifted her into his arms. She was surprised at the surge of relief that flooded through her as she felt his strong arms scoop her up. As much as she hated to admit that he'd been right, she could tell that shock was hitting her, and she knew that the time for trying to prove she was strong was over—realized that the adrenaline rush had indeed been carrying her through the moment.

And now Jack was carrying her through *this* moment.

"Maybe it wouldn't be such a bad idea to head to the hospital," Kat said, her voice shaking. "But no sirens, okay? I really don't want to make a big entrance. This is already embarrassing enough."

"No sirens," he agreed.

He lifted her into the back of the ambulance and nodded to the driver before hopping in himself and closing the doors behind them.

Jack berated himself for agreeing not to use the sirens as he climbed into the back of the ambulance. Kat was probably fine, but she was still a patient in his care and he didn't want any harm to come to her. She was such a typical doctor—assuming she knew best, even when she was the one who needed help.

Of course the first woman he'd been genuinely attracted to in ages would *have* to be a co-worker. And not just any co-worker, but apparently an ambitious and career-driven doctor.

Jack had one hard and fast rule when it came to dating: no doctors. After everything that had happened with Sophie and Matt, he didn't need yet another doctor involved in his personal life. But he couldn't help but notice that the white coat Kat wore over her bikini made her legs look even longer.

None of that kind of thinking, he told himself sternly.

Kat might be attractive, but it would be best for the two of them to put some distance between each another after today.

Although if they were going to be co-workers, distance might not be an option.

He wondered how long she would be at the hospital—what department she would be in. Maybe he wouldn't have to see her that much. He decided to do some casual reconnaissance, hoping she wouldn't pick up on just how curious he really was.

"So you're the new doctor at Oahu General?" he said, as he settled himself across from Kat and pulled out his suturing kit.

But instead of responding, Kat angled her leg away from him. "Oh, no, you don't," she said, as he opened the kit. "The cut's not that bad. It just needs a stitch or two. I could probably do the suturing myself."

Jack glared at her. He had to admire her persistence, but there was such a thing as taking it too far. The fact that Kat would even *suggest* doing stitches on herself told him that she was probably still experiencing some mild shock.

Besides, it would be a crime to allow a scar to form on one of those legs.

"How about you let me be the one to take care of the patient right now?" he said, glowering at her to make sure he'd got his point across.

"It's not as though I can't do a simple stitch," Kat muttered rebelliously.

Jack gently shifted Kat's leg toward his body, so he could reach the cut. He leaned forward and locked her gaze with his. "Listen, I know you were in the top five percent of your class at Northwestern, but I promise you'll be better off if you let *me* handle this," he said. "If you'd stop being so stubborn and let me be in charge for one minute, I'd actually be able to help you."

Kat fell silent, and for a moment Jack regretted his harsh tone. She was probably mortified at the thought of meeting her new co-workers in a few moments, dressed like this. But no, he thought, it was better to be harsh. For her own safety as well as his. *She* needed to accept that she was in the patient's role—a hard thing for a doctor—and *he* needed to make sure that he didn't get carried away by the effect she was having on him. Being clear about maintaining firm professional boundaries from the start would be the best thing for both of them.

Then, in a small voice, Kat muttered, "Top five."

"What?" said Jack.

"I was in the top five of my class at Northwestern. That's much more impressive than being in the top five percent."

He was about to make a sarcastic response, but then, to his surprise, she winked at him.

"I just wanted you to know that I'm a total big shot, okay?" she said.

He couldn't help but laugh. "Noted," he said. *Great,* he thought. *Smart and funny.*

Just what he didn't need. He should keep up a detached, professional demeanor—he really should. But he couldn't help teasing her back.

"With all due respect, Dr. Big Shot, do you think you can relax and let me give this cut the attention it needs?" he asked.

She groaned, startling him.

"What's wrong?" he asked, immediately concerned. "Does it hurt?"

"Oh, no," she said. "It's just...there's that

word again. *Relax.* You keep telling me to do the one thing I have no idea how to do."

"What…relax?"

He started to apply lidocaine to the wound on Kat's leg. He wanted to stay detached, but he couldn't help being curious about her. Besides, if he could keep her talking it would take her mind off the stitches.

"I've never been very good at relaxing," she said. "I've gotten so used to having a busy life that I think I've forgotten how to live in the moment…or maybe I never really knew how. Just before I went down to that beach I thought to myself that I'd learn to relax or die trying. And I guess I almost did."

"*Almost* being the operative word," said Jack. "Not only did you not die, you actually handled yourself really well out there."

"Really?" she said. "Because when you came out there and told me to '*just relax*' that's when I thought we were both doomed for sure."

Jack shook his head. "No, you stayed calm in a terrifying situation. Most people make a rescue more difficult by panicking, but you kept a cool head."

He saw her let out a slow breath that she probably hadn't even realized she was holding.

"I was so scared," she said. "I didn't feel calm at all. I was lucky that you were there."

She had been lucky—that was true enough. Rip currents were incredibly dangerous. But her survival had been more than just luck. Jack had been impressed by how well Kat had stayed focused on his instructions during the rescue, despite her terror.

He started on the first stitch, trying not to notice the thin line of bare skin down her front where her white coat had fallen open.

"You're having an eventful first day in Hawaii," he said. "Do you plan on staying long?"

"Just a year," said Kat. "I used to be an internal medicine doctor at Chicago Grace Memorial, but… I was offered a job here, and…and the timing was good, so I took it."

For a moment Kat seemed sad. Jack wondered what she'd meant about good timing, but he didn't want to pry. If she was only staying for a year, then that meant her appointment at Oahu General was temporary. Maybe he wouldn't even see her that much.

He caught himself noticing how her red hair fell in delicate tendrils around her slender neck and decided that it would probably be for the best if they didn't see each other much.

He said, in what he hoped was a light tone, "You're a visiting doctor? We get a lot of those. What department will you be in?"

"Apparently the infectious diseases department is short-staffed," she said. "They need an internal medicine doctor with a specialty in infectious diseases to head up research and treatment on a new strain of flu."

So she was a doctor of internal medicine? That meant they'd have plenty of opportunities to work together—and he'd have plenty of opportunities to notice the way her hair offset her translucent skin.

He finished the stitches he'd given the cut on Kat's leg. "Infectious Diseases is always short-staffed," he said. "We get new strains of flu every year, and we're always hit by large outbreaks in the spring. It'll be good to have more hands on deck at the hospital." He gave Kat's leg a pat, trying not to think about how her skin felt underneath his fingers. "There," he said brusquely. "Good as new."

With the stitches complete, Jack realized he had no way to distract himself from Kat. There seemed to be nothing to do but sit across from her, trying not to notice that the outline of her body was clear underneath her white coat, which had become damp from the water on her skin.

He cleared his throat. *Stay professional,* he thought to himself. *Right now she's a patient, and even if she wasn't, she's a doctor. You never date doctors.*

Jack decided to keep her talking—both to break the silence, and to distract himself from the way Kat's coat was slipping off one shoulder.

"There aren't too many top med school grads taking jobs at little hospitals in Hawaii," he said.

"It seemed like a good opportunity," she replied.

"Really?" he said. "People usually don't come to the islands to practice medicine unless they've got a personal reason—maybe family lives here, or maybe they grew up in Hawaii and want to move back."

For a moment that expression of sadness crossed her face once again. But then it disappeared just as quickly, to be replaced with cool professionalism. "It was a good opportunity," she repeated. "And I won't just be seeing patients—I've also been offered the chance to lead the internal medicine unit in an administrative role. I'll be able to make some major changes to Oahu General's hospital policy in a way that I've never been able to do at any other hospital before. I wouldn't be able to do that at a larger or more prestigious hospital, so this could be an excellent stepping stone for me."

A stepping stone. This was exactly what irritated Jack about the doctors who came to Hawaii for temporary positions. They were never invested in the islands or the community. They were interested in their careers, and they loved trying out their grand new ideas at a tiny, insignificant hospital where the stakes were low. A tiny, insignificant hospital that happened to be his professional home, with colleagues and patients he cared about.

"Oahu General may not have much prestige, but it's a great hospital, with great doctors," he said.

"Oh, I know," she said quickly. "I didn't mean to imply otherwise. But there's a lot I've learned from working at Chicago Grace Memorial about how to increase efficiency and improve patient outcomes. I'm so excited to start putting some of my ideas in place—I'm sure there's so much that can be improved."

So much that can be improved? thought Jack. She hadn't even seen the hospital yet. How could she know what needed improvement?

It was obvious to him that Kat was a typical big-city doctor, assuming she would be able to change everything. As though the hospital didn't already have good systems in place, built by people who lived in and cared about Hawaii.

His ex-fiancée Sophie had been the same way. Career-driven, independent, and unabashedly pursuing what she wanted from life. They had all been qualities Jack had wholeheartedly admired...until he'd realized that when it came to choosing between her career and the important people in her life Sophie would do whatever it took to advance her career. Even if it meant that people would get hurt.

He'd only known Kat for a few moments, but that was long enough to see that she was smart, funny, beautiful...and completely certain that she knew what was best for everyone.

At least she's only here for a year, he thought. *There's no need for things to get complicated.*

He tried very hard not to notice that Kat's medical coat had fallen open just a little further, revealing another inch of bare, creamy skin. Instead, he focused on packing up the items from his suturing kit, in a manner that he thought was very detached and professional indeed.

Despite Kat's frustration at being treated like a patient, she couldn't help but notice that Jack had handled her stitches swiftly and competently. He clearly knew what he was doing. And as she'd watched Jack complete the stitches she'd felt the soothing effect that observing a simple medical procedure had always had on her.

No matter the emergency, she took comfort in knowing that there was an established process to handle things. Simple injuries like this were almost comforting to face, because it was such a relief to have a plan, to know exactly what to do.

Watching Jack work gave her another chance to appreciate just how muscular his arms were. He'd put his shirt back on when they'd gotten into the ambulance and she wondered if she'd ever be able to get another look at what lay underneath it. But then she sternly guided her thoughts back to the present.

You're still getting over a relationship, she told herself. *You're heartbroken, remember? The last thing you need is to get involved with another guy. Besides, you've already made a fool of yourself in front of this one.*

Her cheeks burned when she recalled how she'd bragged about her accomplishments. She'd only meant to reassure him that she knew what she was doing, but she'd come off sounding so stuck-up. He probably thought she was completely full of herself.

Her body, however, was pushing her in a very different direction than her cool, logical mind.

Do you see how wavy his hair is? her body screamed. *Just run your fingers through it! Do it!*

In the three weeks that had passed since the Day of Doom, Kat had felt an anesthetizing layer of numbness settle over her heartbreak. But the moment she'd taken a good look at Jack something had pierced that and gotten through to the aching heart underneath.

She wasn't ready for it. Feeling attraction to someone wasn't part of this year's plan.

This year's plan was to recover from losing Christopher and losing her job, while learning to embrace life against the serene backdrop of a tropical island setting. Eventually—*much later*—she might start dating again, if the right person came along. But for now it would be completely illogical and inconvenient to feel attracted to anyone. Especially a bossy, over-confident paramedic.

Kat liked her plan. It was a good plan. The thought of deviating from the plan made her nervous. And her attraction to Jack was definitely a deviation, so it would have to stop.

It almost came as a relief when Jack seemed to become increasingly irritated as she discussed her plans for changes at Oahu General Hospital. Dealing with his irritation was much easier than dealing with her feelings of attraction.

Although she couldn't understand what he could possibly be irritated about in the first place.

"Am I missing something?" she said. "Is there some issue with me wanting to make changes at the hospital?"

"Why would there be an issue?" he said.

She didn't buy his innocent act. "I'm not saying there is. But I can't help noticing that you've gotten awfully quiet since I started talking about my job."

"It's just…" He seemed to be choosing his words carefully. "I think you might want to actually get to know the people and the hospital you'll be working at before you start thinking about making any sweeping changes. People can get very set in their way of doing things, and you don't want to push too fast for too much change."

Kat pressed her lips together, trying not to let her emotions show on her face. Jack's words reminded her of what the administrative director at Chicago Grace Memorial Hospital had said, about thirty minutes before she'd been fired.

Kat had spent nearly a year doing research before she'd made her presentation to the hospital board. In it, she had proposed that the hospital open a nonprofit clinic to help provide free and very low-cost care to patients who struggled to afford treatment. She had the financial information to prove the hospital could support it.

All her data indicated that the poorest patients struggled to get well because of their limited resources. They came in to the hospital far too late, after their illnesses had progressed significantly—sometimes too late for help. A non-profit clinic would be life-changing for some of the hospital's patients.

All the board of directors had to do was approve her proposal.

But, to her shock, the administrative director had told her that the hospital was there to make a profit, and that if she wanted to make such sweeping changes she should have gone into politics instead of medicine. She was pushing for too much change, too fast, he'd said. And she'd been stunned to see the other board members nodding in agreement.

And the director had been so condescending and sanctimonious. At one point he had even referred to her as "little lady." His attitude had infuriated her and, unable to stop herself, she'd shared a few choice words with him. The director had fired back, tempers had flared, and before Kat had known it, she'd been out of a job.

When her friend Selena had offered her the job at Oahu General, Kat had been honest about her firing—and the events leading up to it. But no one else knew except for Christopher. And after Christopher's reaction... Well, *that* conversation hadn't gone well at all.

If she could help it no one else would ever know how she'd lost her job. She couldn't reveal to Jack just how much his words had activated her worst fear: that her new plans for the hospital wouldn't work and that her time at Oahu General would lead to a repeat of the Day of Doom.

But that was unlikely to happen again, she reminded herself. This time things were different. She had the full support of the hospital director. And her plans for changes in policy and procedure were good ones... She just needed a chance to prove it. Her year at Oahu General would give her that chance. And if Jack or anyone else had a problem—well, they'd just have to get used to it.

At least she didn't have to worry about losing her job *and* her fiancé on the same day again. After all, she no longer had a fiancé to lose...

She realized her thoughts were hitting too close to emotions she wasn't ready to face. Especially not while she was sitting partially dressed across from a certain dark-haired, half-shaven, irritatingly self-assured paramedic.

"You did that pretty well," she said, indicating her stitches. "You've clearly got some skills." She'd barely felt a thing, and she could already tell she was unlikely to have a trace of a scar.

He looked up at her, seeming surprised by the unexpected compliment.

"You must have gotten lots of practice in the SEALs," she said.

"Actually, I had three years at medical school. So it wasn't exactly a challenge. But it's nice to have my abilities appreciated." He cleared his throat. "You've…um…you've got good skin. So this should heal up very nicely."

His hand was very warm where it rested against her leg. He'd applied the stitches so deftly she tried not to think about anything else his hands might be able to do.

"Three years of medical school would have put you past the worst of it," she said, trying to keep her head clear. "Why didn't you keep going?"

"I happen to love being a paramedic," he said. "I knew medical school wasn't for me, so I left."

Kat was surprised by the defensive tone in Jack's voice. She'd only known him for a few moments, but he struck her as a supremely confident sort of person. Surely he couldn't be sensitive about being a paramedic?

During her career she had met a very small number of physicians with extremely arrogant personalities—her old hospital's administrative director came to mind—who seemed to believe that doctors were somehow superior to other medical professionals. It wasn't a view she agreed with at all. Paramedics and nurses simply provided a different kind of care than doctors. Different and vitally important.

Perhaps Jack had run into a few doctors who held such antiquated views. She hoped he didn't think that she was one of them. But in her pre-hypothermic state, and in her desperation to avoid arriving at Oahu General in an ambulance, she'd probably given him every reason to think that she was as arrogant, stubborn and overconfident as…as *he* was.

"Well, in my opinion you left medical school not a moment too soon," she said lightly.

He looked up at her in surprise.

"If you'd become a doctor you wouldn't have been there on the beach today," she explained. "You wouldn't have been able to save my life. So I'm extremely grateful you decided to become a paramedic instead, no matter what the reason was."

He gave a low, dark laugh. "You're probably the first person who's ever been happy that I left medical school. Well, maybe the second, after me."

There was something more he might have said, Kat could tell. But he didn't speak any further.

Her thoughts turned again to his tattoo. "Are others in your family in the military?" she asked.

"Not exactly," he replied. "My grandfather's

a doctor…as are my parents and both of my brothers."

Ah… Suddenly Jack's defensiveness was a bit more clear. With five doctors in the family, there had probably been many expectations about Jack's career options.

"I knew a few people in medical school whose parents were physicians," she said. "But lots of people don't want to do the same thing as their parents. And I can imagine that being a paramedic in Hawaii would be the best of both worlds to someone who's a former SEAL and a former medical student. You're still able to help people, but you get the rush of adrenaline and excitement that comes with the job."

"Exactly," he said, but again, he didn't elaborate.

I get it, you don't like to talk about the past, she thought. *Duly noted.*

That was fine with her.

She felt the ambulance pull into the hospital docking bay and saw the driver step out. As Jack started to open the back door Kat put her hand on his arm to stop him.

"Wait," she said. "I haven't thanked you properly. If you hadn't been there today I probably would have drowned."

She could tell that he was as surprised as she was by the softness in her voice. What was she *doing*? She had only meant to say thank you, but the emotion behind her voice had been more than just gratitude. And now that she was looking directly at him...now that he was holding her gaze with those ocean-blue eyes...that same electric charge that she'd felt on the beach was there again, keeping her eyes locked with his.

"You mostly saved yourself, by staying calm and trusting my instructions," he said, his voice soft and low. "I was just there to help."

They were by themselves in the back of the ambulance and there was silence. His gaze met hers and Kat couldn't look away. His eyes were pools of cerulean blue. His nose was inches away from hers.

For one insane moment she thought he was going to kiss her—which was a ridiculous idea. Why would Jack want to kiss her? She was a bedraggled mess. And he probably thought she was completely full of herself after she'd bragged about her medical background.

But she'd only bragged because he'd been so bossy at first. So, really, that part was his fault.

And Kat couldn't think why *she* would want a man as irritating as Jack Harper to kiss her.

She only knew that she did.

They were so close. She could smell his sea-salt scent. She felt an undeniable pull toward him, as strong as the current that had pulled her out to sea earlier. But this time, instead of panic, she only felt safety. Calm. A sense of certainty about what would happen next.

But just as his face began moving toward hers, close enough for her to feel the warmth of his breath on her face, two EMTs pulled open the back door of the ambulance.

Kat gave a jump and a start, and she and Jack quickly pulled away from one another. She instantly regretted her sudden move away from Jack, realizing that her reaction would probably make the situation appear even more suspicious to any gossip-prone EMTs. She needed to make it clear to everyone that she and Jack were just co-workers, and she needed to do it quickly.

She pulled the white coat tightly over herself and stepped out of the ambulance. Despite her protests, the EMTs insisted she sit in the wheelchair they'd brought out to meet her.

As they left, she turned back to Jack and said, in her coolest, most professional voice, "It was nice to meet you, Jack. It's good to find out firsthand that I can trust my co-workers to do such a competent job. I think it's great that we'll be working together professionally. Just great."

As Kat was wheeled away Jack let out the long, slow breath that he'd been holding since the driver had stepped out and left the two of them alone together in the ambulance. He had no idea what he'd been thinking in the moment before that almost-kiss with Kat. In fact, he hadn't been thinking at all.

If he had been, he would have been able to tell himself that he and Kat made no sense. That the reasons not to get involved with her far outweighed any attraction he might feel. He ticked them off in his mind. Kat had deliberately emphasized their status as colleagues as she'd left the ambulance. They'd be working together, and workplace relationships were always a mistake. And then there was his most steadfast rule of dating: no doctors.

Not since Sophie. They'd been in medical school together, and then she'd gone on to one prestigious medical research fellowship after another. He'd been fully supportive of her, but when he'd left medical school, she'd let him know in no uncertain terms that she was interested in being the wife of a *doctor*—not a military man or a lowly paramedic.

As hard as it had been to accept, he'd thought he understood. After all, he was the one who had changed, deciding that a doctor's life wasn't for him. He couldn't fault her for wanting something different than what *he* wanted.

But wanting something different was one thing. Finding out that she'd been with his

brother for six months before breaking up with
Jack was quite another.

Sophie had always been extremely ambitious. And Jack's parents were well-known in
the medical field, and the Harper doctors were
a valuable connection.

It was one reason he disliked talking about
his family with others—especially those in the
medical field: he never knew if people were
just trying to get close to him in order to claim
a connection to his family. Had Kat made the
connection? Harper was a common enough last
name, but there weren't many people who had
five doctors in the family. If she did suspect that
his family was essentially medical royalty, she
hadn't said anything.

He'd always wondered if the reason Sophie
had cheated on him with Matt, of all people,
was so that she could still marry into the Harper
family—simply swapping one Harper brother
for another.

Matt, for his part, either hadn't seen it that
way or hadn't cared. Matt had always liked Sophie, Jack knew…but he'd never realized just
how far that attraction went until it was too late.
He'd trusted Sophie. He'd trusted both of them.

Jack didn't want to go through that kind of
heartbreak again. Ever. And as far as he was
concerned he wouldn't have to. There was no

shortage of short-term dating prospects on the islands. Hawaii was full of tourists with romantic ideas about a whirlwind affair before they returned to the mainland. They expected nothing more, and neither did he.

As far as he was concerned love was an illusion, and the best way to protect yourself from heartbreak was to keep from getting close to anyone in the first place.

The more he thought about it, the more he realized that his attraction to Kat wasn't going to be a problem. Kat would only be here for one year. Lots of doctors came to Hawaii for brief appointments—Hawaii's shortage of doctors was well known in the medical community, and visiting doctors weren't rare—but the vast majority of physicians returned to the mainland eventually. Kat seemed like someone who would put her career first, probably over just about anything. She'd leave once she'd gotten over whatever island fantasies she harbored and realized that practicing in Hawaii meant focusing on patient care rather than professional advancement.

He would simply wait out his attraction until she left, and hope that she would forget all about that awkward moment in the ambulance. Which hadn't even been a moment, really. At the time it had felt like an almost-kiss, but now that the moment had passed he realized that she'd probably just meant to express her gratitude. In fact, he might have just completely embarrassed himself by assuming even for an instant that she'd been leaning forward for a kiss.

Yes, she'd been leaning in and turning her face toward him, so close he'd almost been able to count her individual eyelashes...so close he had noticed the tiny freckles dotting her nose, felt her breath on his cheek. But it didn't mean anything. Hell, she might have just been reaching for something.

But he had no intention of asking her about it. That moment in the ambulance was best left forgotten. He'd simply be careful to avoid Kat while they were at work, and then he should have no problem putting her out of his mind. He wouldn't spend any time thinking about that red hair of hers, hanging in dripping ringlets around her neck.

Or the tiny freckles that dotted her nose.

Or her soft, kissable lips.

No, he wouldn't be thinking about any of those things at all.

CHAPTER THREE

"You certainly know how to make an entrance," said Selena.

It was several days after Kat's dramatic first arrival at Oahu General Hospital, and Kat and Selena were sharing coffee in her friend's office. Although they hadn't seen each other in several years, Dr. Selena Kahale had been one of Kat's closest friends when they'd attended medical school together. After Selena had returned to her home in Honolulu, her hard work and natural warmth had helped her to climb the ranks quickly to become clinical director of Oahu General Hospital.

But apparently her esteemed professional position didn't get in the way of teasing an old friend.

Kat blushed, remembering the amount of good-natured ribbing she'd endured as soon as the EMTs had learned who she was. Despite her protestations that she was fine, they had insisted on wheeling her into an exam room, still wet, with her medical coat wrapped around her concealing her bikini.

"I wasn't planning on showing up on my first day dressed like that," said Kat, completely embarrassed.

Selena might be an old friend, but she was now Kat's boss, and Kat wasn't sure how she'd view the whole incident.

She let out a breath of relief when Selena said, "Relax. It's Hawaii. No one stands on ceremony here. You'll find things are much more informal than what you're probably used to back in Chicago. Tommy Bahama shirts are basically considered formalwear. My only worry is whether you'll be able to get used to how casual things are around here."

"It's certainly a big change," said Kat.

That was an understatement. The environment at Oahu General Hospital was sometimes so casual that she was taken aback. After her first day she'd scrapped any thoughts of showing up in a power suit—she would have felt ridiculous wearing a formal blazer here.

Back at Chicago Grace there had been a clear hierarchy among the staff, and everyone had known where they stood. Kat had often wondered if the culture of strict adherence to authority there had interfered with patient care, since some of the doctors were too afraid to question a senior physician's diagnosis, or to make changes to treatment plans that their supervisors might disagree with.

But at Oahu General Hospital the atmosphere felt completely different. Everyone seemed to genuinely respect one another, regardless of hierarchy. Doctors routinely took advice from nurses and paramedics, everyone's input seemed to be valued, and there was an easy banter among the staff.

This relaxed atmosphere presented her with a new challenge. In Chicago, whenever she'd acted as the attending physician, her team had listened to her and carried out her instructions because she was in charge. Simply being in a position of authority had been enough for her team to respect her. But here in Hawaii she saw she would have to earn the respect of her colleagues, as well as their trust.

Selena seemed to sense her thoughts. "Every hospital's culture is a little different," she said. "Even I was a little taken aback by the informality here at first, and I grew up on the islands. But I've come to realize that Oahu General is a special place. We're like family here. You'll grow to love it, I'm sure. And I know that everyone will love you too. Just give them time to get to know you."

Selena paused to sip her coffee, and then continued.

"You might be surprised at how well you fit in here if you can just give yourself time to adjust. The Kat Murphy I remember from medical school was so idealistic, so committed to making a difference in her patients' lives. Maybe getting sacked from Chicago Grace was a blessing in disguise."

Kat blinked. "What kind of blessing involves spending a year doing research for a proposal that ultimately fails?"

"Think about it," said Selena. "Chicago Grace Memorial may be one of the most prestigious hospitals in the country, but ultimately it's a for-profit hospital. The Kat I know could never be completely happy working at a hospital where patients are seen based on their ability to pay. That's not you. It's not where you come from."

Kat mulled this over. She and Selena had been close friends at medical school, and Selena knew how important it was to Kat to use medicine to make a difference. But when Kat had first begun working at Chicago Grace she'd been so excited about the hospital's reputation and the research opportunities it provided that she hadn't thought much about how the hospital's values might differ from her own.

As she'd continued working there it had become impossible not to see the truth in front of her: there were too many patients who couldn't afford the care they needed.

She knew how that felt.

When she was growing up her parents had always waited until the last possible minute to seek medical care. Even as a child Kat had understood that money was tight in her family. Although her parents had always taken her to see a doctor promptly when she was ill, she knew that they'd often put off their own medical care in order to save money.

Then, when she was ten, her father had come down with an illness. "Just a cold," he had said, reassuring Kat and her mother.

When the cold had persisted he'd said it must just be the flu, and that he would see a doctor when he had time to take a break from his job. He'd kept telling them that he would see a doctor in just a few days. A few weeks later, the flu had turned into pneumonia, and by then her father's condition had been severe. He'd passed away just one day after being admitted to a hospital.

So it wasn't enough for Kat simply to be a good doctor. It hadn't been enough simply to work at Chicago Grace, with all its glamour and prestige. She wanted to make a real difference in the medical community. And more than anything she wanted to make sure that no child, no family, had to go through what she'd gone through as a little girl.

Which was why she had wanted the director of Chicago Grace Memorial to accept her proposal to open a nonprofit clinic at the hospital. It would have been her chance to finally make a true difference—a contribution to medicine that came directly from her personal experience and her professional values.

She had thought that ultimately the board of directors—many of them physicians themselves—would agree that any impact on the hospital's profits would be a small price to pay for a vast increase in quality of patient care.

How naïve she'd been.

Instead of simply rejecting Kat's proposal, the board members had expressed deep indignation at her research findings, which had shown that wealthier patients recovered faster than poorer patients. They'd complained that her findings were terrible for the public's view of the hospital, and they'd told her to bury all her data.

Kat had refused, and it had been that refusal, as well as the choice words she had exchanged with the hospital director, that had resulted in her being fired.

She'd finally had her chance to make a difference and she'd failed. She hadn't been able to convince the hospital board to open a nonprofit clinic. She hadn't been able to control her temper when the hospital director had been condescending and rude. And she hadn't been able to make Christopher understand why all of it was so important to her.

She'd expected his support, but instead he'd seemed just as shocked as the hospital board members. Instead of sharing her anger he'd been angry with Kat, for exchanging insults with the hospital director.

"How could you?" he'd said. *"You might as well have thrown away your career."*

She'd been furious with him. Devastated and furious.

Tears pricked as she remembered their conversation and how cold he'd been. She stared into her coffee mug, hoping Selena wouldn't see those tears that still sprang to her eyes whenever Christopher came to mind.

"You know, as glad as I am to have you here, I was a little surprised when you took the job," Selena said. "Hawaii's so far from Chicago. I would have thought you'd try to look for something a little closer to your family."

"I needed a change," Kat said. "A big change."

The last thing she wanted to admit to her old friend was that she'd moved to Hawaii because of the breakup. It was such a cliché. And Selena would expect her to be professional.

She took a deep breath and tried to think of how she could explain in a way that Selena would understand. But before she could start Selena said, "It was the breakup with Christopher, wasn't it?"

Kat choked on her coffee in surprise. "How did you know?"

"Come on, Kat! *Three days* before the wedding you post online that it's over? And then there's complete radio silence from you—none of your friends can get in touch with you. That's not just a breakup—that's a broken heart."

"I don't want you to think I moved here just because of what happened with…with him," Kat said. It was still too hard to say Christopher's name. "I'm serious about this job—I'm not here just to get over a guy."

"You think I don't understand that? I'm a single mom—I know exactly how it feels to have your life change completely and unexpectedly. You don't have to go through this alone."

Didn't she? Kat was glad to have Selena's support, but now that she was nearing the end of her first week in Hawaii she was beginning to realize that she felt more alone than she ever had in her life.

Now that the excitement of moving to the

island was wearing off, Kat felt as though she wasn't sure who she was. She wasn't a top internal medicine doctor at one of the most prestigious hospitals in the country. She wasn't Christopher's fiancée—she definitely wasn't his wife. And she wasn't living in Chicago, the city where her family and friends lived, where she'd planned to spend the rest of her life.

For as long as she could remember she'd tried to be the best doctor on the staff, the best fiancée to Christopher. But if she wasn't trying to prove herself to anyone then how did she know who she was supposed to be?

Kat blinked back tears, willing her eyes to dry. "The point is, it's in the past," she said. "I came here to try to let go of him…of everything that was holding me back. But I just don't know what I'm supposed to do next."

"Oh, Kat." Selena set her coffee aside and patted Kat's shoulder tenderly. "I think you really have come to the right place." Then she gave Kat a wicked smile. "And it looks like you're already making friends. Didn't one of Oahu's most eligible bachelors fish you out of the Pacific recently?"

"Eligible bachelors? Are you talking about Jack Harper?"

"Who else? If you wanted to meet him you

didn't have to nearly drown yourself—I could have set you up on a date."

"Selena! I am *so* not ready to date yet. One of the reasons I came here was to try to learn how to slow down and relax."

Selena raised an eyebrow. "Forgive me for being skeptical, but I don't think 'slow down and relax' is a phrase I've *ever* heard you use."

"Maybe I don't have the strongest reputation in that respect, but I'm trying to change that," said Kat. "I'm trying to let go of the past and do something new. Which means I'm definitely not looking to get romantically involved with anyone right now. And even if I was, Jack and I aren't right for one another."

"Okay, first of all, you *are* ready to date—you just don't know it. You've already completed the first essential step to getting over a breakup."

"Which is?"

"Getting out of the continental U.S. as quickly as possible. Now you need to move on to step two: the rebound. And for that purpose Jack is *perfect* for you."

Kat swallowed. How much did Selena know of the kiss that had almost happened between her and Jack? Had the EMTs decided that their brief glimpse of Jack and a half-clothed Kat in close quarters was gossip-worthy after all?

She responded carefully. "I'm not so sure I'd

say he's *perfect* for me. He seems pretty bossy. And even if I were interested—which I'm not—he probably doesn't want anything to do with me."

"Why on earth would you say that?" said Selena. "From what I heard, you two were getting pretty cozy just around the time the ambulance pulled up to the hospital."

Damn, thought Kat. So there *had* been gossip. She needed to set the record straight with Selena as soon as possible. What had happened with Jack—or what had almost happened—had just been a misunderstanding, nothing more.

"I don't know what people have been saying, but Jack was simply taking care of the cut on my leg. Both of us were completely professional. We did get to know each other a little…"

"And?" said Selena, rapt with anticipation.

"And I don't think I'm his type. We kind of got off on the wrong foot. I hate to admit it, but I don't think I made the best first impression—I may have sounded a little full of myself. I blame the hypothermia. And I think—no, I'm *sure*—Jack would agree that since we're to be co-workers it's best not to let emotions get in the way of our working together."

Selena waved her hand dismissively. "Honey, that's all *relationship* stuff. What you need is a *fling.*"

"I'm not really sure I'm a fling kind of girl."

Selena narrowed her eyes. "Kat. Sweetheart. Did you not hear me say that I'm a single mother? When I'm not working, my days involve making lunches and spending way too much time discussing purple crayons with a toddler whom I love to pieces but who has barely mastered words of two syllables. I need some excitement. I need to live vicariously through someone else's love-life. And I need you to be that person because I don't have time for that kind of drama myself!"

Kat laughed. "Sorry, but my love-life's never been all that exciting. If you're looking for vicarious thrills you'll have to look somewhere else."

"Oh, come *on*!" said Selena. "I thought you came here to let go of the past and try new things?"

"Well, yes, but... I'm not sure I want Jack Harper to be one of those 'new things.'"

"Why not? Jack is great. And he's ideal for you right now because he's not a relationship kind of guy. Don't get me wrong—he's a good person. And I love working with him. He's great at his job, really funny, and a good friend. But he's tailor-made fling material; he never dates *anyone* for long."

"I'll just bet he doesn't," said Kat through

gritted teeth. Selena was simply confirming her first impression of him.

Selena continued to gush about Jack's virtues.

"He's a lot like you, actually," she said. "He could have worked anywhere on the mainland, but he chose to come here instead. And he's not just *any* paramedic. His parents are *the* Harpers—from the University of Nebraska in Lincoln—"

"Wait a minute," said Kat.

Jack *Harper?* It was quite a common last name and she hadn't given it a second thought till now.

"You mean his parents are Michael and Janet Harper? The famous research scientists? I still have some of their books from medical school on my shelf."

She remembered Jack had touched on the subject of his family in the ambulance, and now knew her feeling that he'd been holding something back had been spot-on. She couldn't understand how he could have talked about his family without ever mentioning that his parents were famous in the medical world.

"What the hell is the son of two of the most well-known medical researchers in the country doing working as a paramedic at a small hospital in Hawaii?" she asked.

"Shouldn't you be asking yourself a similar question?" Selena's eyes twinkled. "What's one of the most respected internists in the U.S. doing at my little hospital? I'm sure he has his reasons, just as you do. You see? You two *are* a lot alike."

"Sure, if oil and water are alike…" Kat muttered.

"I don't know why he wants to work here, but I'm glad he does," Selena continued. "He's a gifted paramedic. Most of the patients he brings in are already stable by the time they get to the hospital, no matter what the emergency."

"Yes, I could tell he was very competent. But I made it clear to him that I was a doctor and he still flat-out ignored me and did everything his own way."

"You're too used to medical hierarchy," Selena told her. "Here we're more egalitarian. We make our decisions with everyone's input rather than automatically deciding that whoever's in charge knows best. It's a team approach. It takes some getting used to, but it's one of the things I love most about practicing here. And I think you'll learn to love it, too."

Selena's eyes grew mischievous.

"And maybe you'll fall in love with something else as well. Some*one* else…with blue eyes and dark hair and—"

"Oh, my God, Selena, let it go!" Kat held up one of the sofa pillows, threatening to throw it at her friend. "Jack and I are *not* going to happen. Maybe if he were the last man on this island I'd consider it. But only then."

Selena's eyes twinkled. "We'll see," she said. "It's a pretty small island."

Kat cleared her throat. "Is there perhaps something we can discuss *besides* my love-life? Something involving medicine?"

"Right!" said Selena. "The whole reason you're here. The virus outbreaks."

Selena sat behind her desk and pulled out several files for Kat to examine.

"Because of its location, Hawaii is vulnerable to all the strains of virus that sweep through Asia, so we try to keep an eye on what's happening there in order to be prepared for what could happen here."

She drew Kat's attention to one of the files.

"We're calling this one H5N7. There have been a few isolated cases on Oahu. Catching the signs early and keeping people quarantined to prevent the spread of infection has been key. But our hospital is too small to handle a major infectious disease event. My biggest worry is that a larger outbreak would strain our resources to such an extent that we wouldn't be able to provide effective care to patients who would otherwise be cured."

Kat nodded. "On the mainland you can rely on the resources of other hospitals, but here you can't simply call in for reinforcements or send your overflow of patients to another hospital nearby."

"Exactly. Sending patients to hospitals on the other islands can be a huge hassle. And even if we could, the only Level One trauma center for all the islands is located right here in *our* hospital—there's two thousand miles of ocean between us and the next nearest one. So we're observing very strict contamination procedures with any patient who comes in."

Kat passed the files back to Selena. "As far as I can tell you're doing the best you can to stay ahead of this thing," she said. "What's the status of any potential vaccine?"

"We're working with a team at the University of Hawaii at Manoa to see what can be done. So far their results are promising. In the meantime we're following the strictest quarantine procedures for any patients brought into the hospital with signs of flu, or any health workers who have been exposed. That means full haz-mat gear when we're working with affected patients. I've put a policy in place stating that any hospital staff members who come into contact with potentially infected patients will be housed here at the hospital, in a secure holding area, until we can confirm whether or not they've been exposed to the illness. If blood tests do confirm exposure, then it's a mandatory 10-day quarantine so that we have time to observe whether symptoms manifest, and so we can start treatment immediately if necessary. Bottom line, make sure you're taking the standard universal precautions with every patient, but be on the lookout for the rash and other symptoms so that you can be extra-careful with affected patients. So far, none of our staff have been exposed yet, and I intend to keep it that way."

Kat nodded. "Like I say, sounds like you're doing everything you can."

"We are," said Selena, "but I feel better now that you're here." Selena squirmed uncomfortably. "Actually…you may have to communicate quite a bit with Jack on this."

"Why? He's a paramedic."

"Exactly. If the outbreaks do increase, paramedics and EMTs will be at the greatest risk. They're the ones who will be exposed to the victims first. So it's essential that they keep us abreast of any risk of the flu spreading because they'll be the first to know."

Kat sighed. It seemed that avoiding Jack Harper would be harder than she'd thought.

* * *

After several weeks Kat began to settle into a rhythm at the hospital. She worked with the researchers from the University of Hawaii on the flu virus and shared ER shifts with the other doctors. They were a relaxed, easygoing bunch. And as Kat got used to the hospital's informality she began to appreciate the casual atmosphere.

She made friends with Kimo, the shift coordinator, who would bring in extra *kalua* pork sandwiches his mother had made. She got to know Marceline, a cardiologist, who would regale Kat with lurid stories of her former life as a webcam girl. "Modeling" skimpy outfits in front of her computer had helped Marceline pay for most of medical school. And one of the surgeons, Omar, was rumored to be royalty in his home country, but he was very clandestine about it. Kat had the feeling that he allowed the rumor to continue because it added to his air of mystery and seemed to improve his dating prospects quite a bit.

It was a colorful cast of characters, and nothing at all like the strait-laced, buttoned-up doctors she'd worked with back home.

The patients were different, too. Kat was used to seeing patients who were seeking second or third opinions on the prognosis of serious or rare illnesses. People came to Chicago Grace Memorial Hospital when other physicians had reached the end of their knowledge and were unable to provide more guidance, and Kat had typically used her expertise there to make hard-to-call diagnoses of illnesses that were extremely rare or difficult to treat.

Oahu General Hospital ran itself more like a small general practice. She saw children who had stuck innumerable crayons up their noses, and tourists with sprains or fractures because they'd taken risks while hiking.

She also saw entirely too much of Jack.

Somehow she always seemed to be on shift when he was bringing in patients. As if that wasn't bad enough he seemed to be constantly flirting—with everyone except Kat. Every time Kat saw him he was flashing his hundred-watt smile at the receptionists, or sharing private jokes with the nurses, or twinkling his eyes at patients.

She wasn't sure why Jack's behavior should bother her so much. She didn't care who he flirted with. After all, she wasn't interested in him, and he wasn't interested in her. She simply felt that one should maintain a professional attitude at work. A casual atmosphere was all well and good, but people could take these things too far. There was no need for Jack to go winking his ocean-blue eyes at everyone in sight, or giving his bright white smile to every woman who crossed his path.

Good God, she thought one day, when Jack smiled at a nurse who'd helped him lift a heavy patient off a gurney. *Even his teeth are perfect.*

It was all very distracting. And that was the problem, thought Kat. Jack's flirting with other people didn't bother her the least little bit. It was simply annoying to be constantly distracted by his tanned skin or his muscular arms. Why did he have to wear such tight shirts?

She'd tried to avoid him, but working at such a small hospital made it difficult to avoid anyone. He brought her just as many cases as he brought the other doctors—if not more. But he seemed to delight in bringing her the most ridiculous cases he could find. And then he wouldn't simply leave, the way most paramedics did. Every time he brought in a case, he would linger, as though he wanted to see how she would handle things.

When she'd challenged him on it he'd claimed that he was merely staying nearby in case she needed additional assistance. She didn't believe him for a minute. She was certain that he was sticking around so he could watch her reaction—which, in her opinion, proved that he was bringing her preposterous cases on purpose.

She dealt with it the only way she knew

how—by maintaining a distant, cool, professional demeanor. And for his part Jack seemed to have no trouble keeping his face completely deadpan. Even today, as he pulled back one of the ER privacy curtains to reveal a young couple on a gurney. The woman sat upright, and her boyfriend was lying on his side.

Kat listened to their story.

"So where are you saying the zucchini is now?" she asked patiently.

After the couple had left, with a treatment plan and some stern words of warning about the inadvisability of placing vegetables in bodily orifices, Kat grabbed Jack and pulled him behind the curtain.

"I know what you're doing and it needs to stop," she hissed.

He blinked at her innocently. "I'm just doing my job. It's not my fault if I'm bringing patients to the ER while you happen to be on shift."

"There are other doctors on shift! Find one of them! The other day you had an acute appendicitis case and you brought it to Omar. But what kinds of cases do you bring *me*? College students who stick vegetables God knows where! A toddler who's pushed thirteen marbles up his nose! An elderly woman with dementia who ate all the little cakes her granddaughter made from Play-Doh because she thought they were real!"

"Hey, I thought she was sweet."

"She *was* sweet! That's not the point. You're doing this on purpose!"

"Doing what on purpose?" he asked innocently.

"Giving all the weird cases to me."

He shook his head. "Why on earth would I do that?" he said.

"I have no idea. Don't ask me what the motives of a sociopath are. But I've got news for you, pal. I've seen just about every crazy ER case in the book. Marbles are nothing—you wouldn't believe some of the things I've seen kids stick up their noses. You're not going to shock me with anything."

He held his hands up. "I believe you—I'm sure that you're unshockable. But I swear I'm not doing this on purpose. You've had a run of strange cases lately, I'll admit, but I promise I'm just bringing the patients as they come in."

As he spoke Kat realized just how close she and Jack were in physical proximity to one another. What had she been thinking when she pulled him behind a curtain? They could have had this conversation in public. Once again she'd ended up getting herself caught in close quarters with Jack. How did that keep happening?

She yanked open the curtain, deciding that

it would be best to get out of the enclosure as quickly as possible—but she was stopped short by the small crowd of hospital staff that had gathered just outside.

There were several orderlies, as well as Marceline, Kimo and Omar. They tried to act casual, but they'd clearly been listening to her argument with Jack. *Great*, thought Kat. If their moment in the ambulance hadn't been enough, then rumors would definitely be flying about the two of them after this.

Jack really wasn't trying to hand off the most bizarre patients to Kat—it was simply a matter of bad timing. He knew they'd gotten off on the wrong foot. But he wasn't used to having his decisions questioned or challenged while he was trying to save lives. And yet, as argumentative and challenging as Kat had been, there was a strong air of feistiness about her that he admired. She didn't seem like someone who gave up easily, whatever the circumstances.

He might have come off as bossy, but hadn't Kat acted the same way? He had been trying to provide her with medical care, while she'd been trying to convince him that she knew best by waving her credentials in front of his face—as though she couldn't possibly trust his expertise over her own.

Did she think he should be impressed by her credentials rather than her competence? It was the same kind of thinking he'd often noticed among his family members, who seemed to value the achievements and connections of medical professionals more than the skill they demonstrated.

Now that he'd spent a few weeks working with Kat he could tell that she was one of the most competent doctors he'd ever worked with. But he'd had no way of knowing that before.

And, just as he'd thought, Kat had started trying to implement changes at the hospital right away. Some changes had gone down better than others. First she'd required the EMTs and paramedics to switch from a three-point to a five-point triage system, and even he had to admit that it had been a *good* change. But her most controversial decision had been to ask all hospital staff to spend eight hours a month working at the hospital's nonprofit walk-in clinic.

Granted, she'd adjusted everyone's schedules so that this didn't impact too much on anyone's working hours.

But, while he might be able to acknowledge that Kat's changes so far were an improvement on an intellectual level, he still felt frustrated. Kat's ideas might be good, but that wasn't the point. The point was that she was a big-city doctor who thought she could just walk into a little hospital—*his* little hospital—and turn his job and his emotions upside down.

At first he'd tried to keep his distance, to give his feelings a chance to subside. But, if anything, avoiding Kat had seemed to intensify his attraction toward her, and he'd constantly found himself wondering how she was adjusting to her new job, whether she was talking to the other staff members, or if she was wearing that green blouse that offset her eyes so well.

To make matters worse, as he continued to work with Kat he became increasingly certain that he wasn't just attracted to her—he *liked* her as well. She had a wry sense of humor, and she seemed to possess wells of infinite patience and compassion with even the most difficult patients. She had a warm and ready smile, and she smiled often—just not at him.

So he'd decided to change tactics. Instead of avoiding Kat, he'd started to make a point of being sure to acknowledge her each time their paths crossed. He'd been trying to keep their encounters polite and casual. But that strategy had become more complicated when the hospital had suddenly been hit with a run of cases that bordered on the absurd.

Jack wasn't surprised that Kat thought he was bringing her weird cases on purpose, but he wished there was a way to convince her that it was just a coincidence that her caseload of late had been a bit unusual.

At least she'd never brought up their almost-kiss in the ambulance. His hunch was that she was just as eager to put that incident behind them as he was. He wondered if it would be possible for them to have a fresh start. The sooner he could convince her that he wasn't bringing her strange cases on purpose—that he did not, in fact, have any special interest in her, in any way—the sooner he could start trying to convince himself of the same thing.

He wasn't quite sure how, but he'd find a way.

A few days later, the doors of the elevator in the hospital's parking garage were just closing in front of Kat when a hand reached out to stop them. They automatically shifted open again, and Kat was surprised to see Jack standing in front of her.

"May I?" he said, motioning inside the elevator.

Kat shrugged. "Plenty of room," she said.

He got onto the elevator with her, and they began their ascent from the basement to the trauma unit. But Jack surprised Kat again by pushing the emergency stop button.

Before she could speak, he said, "Look, I

know we got off on the wrong foot, and I just wanted to clear the air. Back in the ambulance, I...um..."

Oh, no, thought Kat. Was Jack was about to bring up their almost-kiss? She needed to take control of this conversation, and fast.

"I was a jerk," she said quickly. "You were just trying to help, and I argued and fought you every step of the way. I blame the hypothermia. You were just doing your job."

"That's true," he said. "But I have to admit that I'm not used to treating patients who have medical experience...just like you probably weren't used to being in the patient's role."

He was trying to offer her an olive branch. Maybe she should take it. They did have to work together, after all. She'd tried desperately to deal with her attraction by avoiding him, but that strategy didn't seem to be working. If anything, she thought about him more than ever.

Maybe the problem was that she wasn't seeing Jack as a real person. The distance between them was causing her to focus too much on his physical attractiveness. Maybe if she spent more time with him, got to know him as a normal person whom she had to see every day, whom she had to work with, then he'd lose some of his luster. This man with his dark, wavy hair and perfect teeth was sure to have some flaws—she simply hadn't been around him enough to notice any of them. Maybe once she discovered a few of them her heart and stomach would stop doing flip-flops every time she saw him.

And it would be nice to stop being so distracted by his scent, as well. How did he always manage to smell like the beach? It filled the elevator now—the scent of sunblock, saltwater, and pure masculinity. Maybe she'd get desensitized if she were around him enough…

"I really haven't been bringing you the weird cases on purpose," he was saying. "I don't know why all of the odd ones have been coming in during your ER shifts, but I promise I haven't been giving them to you intentionally."

"Hmm…" she said. "Not even that toddler who swallowed the voice box from his teddy bear, and we could all hear Teddy's disembodied voice coming out of the kid's lower abdomen every time he pressed on his stomach?"

"*Especially* not that one." Jack shuddered. "That was creepy."

Suddenly Kat found herself laughing. The case really had been ridiculous. And anyway, even if he *had* been bringing her odd cases on purpose, dealing with the unexpected was part of the job.

His relief at her laughter seemed sincere, so Kat thought that his apology probably was as well. "All right, Jack," she said. "How about a truce?"

And finally—*finally*—after all this time, she found herself the recipient of his smile. The full force of it was just as dazzling as she had known it would be. Her knees felt a little weak, but she managed to casually grip the bar on one side of the elevator, as though she were just shifting her stance.

"A truce sounds good," he said. "I have a feeling that if we're not bickering we might actually find out we like working together."

Kat wasn't sure what to say.

Certainly not, *I'd like that, but I'm very attracted to you, and that's really interfering with my ability to recover from a fiancé who practically left me at the altar just a few weeks ago.*

No, that response was probably off the table.

She settled for giving him a small smile instead.

He released the emergency stop button and the elevator began moving upward again. This would be good, thought Kat. They would get to know each other a little better, and soon enough she'd get used to him. He'd never need to know how badly she wanted to run her fingers through his dark hair.

When the elevator doors opened on the trauma

unit all was in chaos. Even Selena was sweeping around the ER floor, conducting triage.

She nodded at Jack and Kat as they stepped out of the elevator. "Major car crash on the expressway," she said, by way of explanation. "We've got multiple trauma cases coming in at once. Grab one and get to work."

Jack and Kat nodded at one another. At the end of the hallway a team of EMTs were wheeling a gurney with an incoming patient on it toward the ER; Kat rushed toward them, with Jack close behind her.

"What've we got?" Kat asked Marco, the head EMT on duty.

"Man who looks to be in his late fifties with multiple fractures. His breathing was shallow when we first picked him up, but now he's not breathing at all. He got smashed up pretty bad in the expressway crash. We had to use the jaws of life to get him out from under his car."

"How long has he been unresponsive?"

"Less than a few seconds."

"His pulse is thready," said Jack. "Could be something obstructing the airway."

Kat placed her stethoscope on the man's chest. She could hear a heartbeat, but there were no sounds of respiration. "We'll need to intubate," she said. "Let's get him to an operating room."

She was about to ask Jack if he'd be able to

come with her, but he'd already moved to the other side of the gurney and was helping her push it down the hallway.

"Thanks," she said breathlessly as she tried to keep pace with him. "I know they need you out there."

"You need me in here," he responded as they pushed the patient's gurney into the OR.

He immediately began attending to the pulse oximeter, and Kat was relieved to see there was no need to talk him through the procedure; he'd clearly done this before.

Before she could ask, he handed her a laryngoscope. Kat tilted the patient's head back and inserted the scope into his mouth, taking care to avoid the man's teeth. As she pushed the endotracheal tube into the patient's airway Jack began to inflate the balloon that would deliver air into his lungs. He continued inflations as Kat positioned her stethoscope first above one lung and then the other, to listen for sounds of respiration.

There.

Kat relaxed her shoulders as she identified the ragged but unmistakable sound of breathing in both lungs. They'd need an X-ray to ensure correct placement of the tube, but hearing respiration from both lungs meant that the patient should stabilize quickly.

She straightened up from where she was bent over the patient and looked at Jack in astonishment. "I don't think I've ever gotten a line into a patient so fast," she said.

He flashed a smile at her and Kat felt another pang. Just a few minutes ago she'd been hoping that spending more time with Jack would help desensitize her to his charm. But now, finding that they were able to work together so seamlessly... Kat thought she might actually *want* to work with Jack more often if it meant that her medical procedures would go this smoothly.

If she could just get her heart to stop going into overdrive every time he smiled they'd be a great team.

"One of the easiest intubations I've ever done," he agreed, looking at the patient's pulse-ox levels on the monitor. "I'd say we should take him down to X-Ray to ensure correct placement of the line, but..."

"What is it?" said Kat.

"Come look."

Kat came around to Jack's side of the gurney and was suddenly filled with dread.

The distinctive rash of the super-flu was spread over the man's legs and abdomen: small red bumps. And she and Jack had been working on him without haz-mat suits, and with only standard levels of protection between the two of them.

Kat realized that her plan to take the edge off her attraction to Jack by getting to know him better was about to blow up in her face.

She was going to get to know Jack better, all right. Kat remembered what Selena had told her about the hospital's policy regarding virus exposure.

Kat looked at Jack's face, and knew what he was thinking, too.

They might be about to spend a long time together.

CHAPTER FOUR

KAT AND JACK had only been in the secure holding room for a few hours before Kat was certain of one thing: no matter how much time they spent together, she was never going to become desensitized to Jack Harper.

She'd wondered if being quarantined with Jack would let the two of them get to know each other better. But she quickly realized he was as guarded as ever when she mentioned that the research team working on the virus had been using studies conducted by his parents for reference. She'd only meant to reassure him that she thought the team was close to developing a vaccine, but his reaction surprised her.

"Look," he said, "I deal with this every time we get a new doctor at the hospital, so I'm just going to tell you this now: I haven't spoken with any of my family members for more than four years. So if you're trying to wangle an introduction to any of the great Dr. Harpers, you're barking up the wrong tree."

"What?" said Kat, surprised. "Jack, you've totally got the wrong idea. I just meant that your parents' research has been extremely useful."

When he still looked skeptical, Kat went on.

"Selena mentioned your family during my first few days here. What I don't understand is why it should be any sort of secret. If I came from a family like yours I'd be telling everyone. With those kinds of connections in the medical field—"

"Connections with the Harpers are only useful if you're doing what they want you to do," he said. "If you're trying to forge your own path, then being a member of the Harper family is more of a liability than an advantage."

Kat nodded slowly. "I'm guessing they didn't love it that you dropped out of medical school."

"That about sums it up," he said.

She wanted to ask him more, but she could see that the subject was closed.

Why did he have to smell so good? Her plan—the plan that had sounded so good in her mind earlier that morning—was not going to work.

She'd had high hopes that if she could simply spend more time with Jack she might start to think of him as a normal person, instead of someone she felt unaccountably attracted to. But the more time she spent with Jack, the more tantalizing he became. The question of whether his eyes were blue, or more of a deep sea-green, was becoming a matter of some urgency to her, as she found her mind wandering back to his eyes anytime she tried to concentrate.

She and Jack had been housed together in a small room at the far end of the hospital's rarely used west wing. Selena had apologized for the small size of the designated isolation area and had made a halfhearted offer to try to find a way to provide separate rooms for them, but Kat could tell her friend was concerned about the hospital's limited capacity due to the influx of patients from the highway crash. Kat and Jack had both reassured Selena that they would be fine sharing a single room with privacy curtains, although secretly Kat wasn't thrilled at the idea, and from the expression on his face, she could tell that Jack felt the same way. But if sharing a room with Jack would help to make room for more patients, then Kat would cope with the situation the best she could.

Selena had arranged for the infectious disease team to run blood tests on the affected patient. It would take anywhere from a few hours to a few days to be sure. If the team confirmed that the patient did have the super-flu, then Kat and

Jack would be spending at least the next ten days together, to ensure that neither of them showed any sign of having contracted the virus.

Kat hoped with all her heart that the patient didn't have the virus—both for the patient's sake and because she wasn't sure how she was going to be able to sleep knowing Jack was a mere two feet away from her.

The room was sparse: it contained two gurneys with privacy curtains, a shared bathroom, and an old television set that could access about three network channels. With their limited entertainment options Kat could tell that it was going to be a long ten days, if it came to that.

It didn't help that their close quarters only served to highlight how different they were from one another. She could tell by the way that Jack had haphazardly thrown his belongings about the room that he was the kind of person who didn't seem to mind clutter. She, on the other hand, preferred things to be neat and orderly—even if they would only be staying there for a few days.

"We should decide which parts of the room are yours and which are mine," she said. Maybe keeping their things to separate areas would help her to ignore the mess.

He blinked, looking around the tiny, five-hundred-square-foot room. "Isn't that kind of irrelevant in a room this small?" he said. "I don't think there's much we can do to avoid each other's space."

Kat gritted her teeth. She had a feeling that she wanted to tolerate his clutter about as much as he wanted to talk about his family.

"Some people might say that in a tiny space it's even *more* important to be clear about what goes where," she said.

"Fine," he replied. "How about I stay on my gurney and you stay on yours, and the rest can work itself out?"

She took a deep breath.

You're learning how to relax, she reminded herself. *You're learning how to let go and live in the moment. Maybe this is your chance to practice that.*

The Old Kat would have insisted on trying to win the argument. The New Kat was going to disengage.

She unpacked a small mountain of meditation workbooks and arranged them at the foot of her gurney in a neat stack, making sure they were organized by subject and author's last name. If she had to be in quarantine she might as well use her time productively.

When Selena had heard about Kat's mission to spend the year learning how to relax she'd provided Kat with an extensive collection of self-help workbooks, meditation recordings, and podcasts on mindfulness. Selena had termed the project "Operation Rebound," while Kat preferred to think of it as "Operation Inner Peace." She'd gotten through about a third of the workbooks, but inner peace was still proving elusive.

Learning to relax was a much more daunting task than she'd originally thought.

The key to achieving a relaxed state, according to all of her meditation recordings and workbooks, was to practice putting aside distracting thoughts in order to turn her mind to the present moment. So she sat on her gurney with her legs crossed and her eyes closed as a soothing voice through her headphones instructed her. And she tried to follow the instructions—she really did.

First she turned aside all thoughts about Jack's eyes.

Then she turned aside all thoughts about his hair, and what it might feel like to run her fingers through it.

Then she turned aside her thoughts about whether that tantalizing scent of his might have a bit of sandalwood in it. Was the smell just *him*, she wondered, or did he put on some sort of cologne?

It was strange, she thought, that she didn't have to try very hard to keep her mind off Christopher. It was Christopher who'd broken her heart, after all. Just three days before their wedding. Her heart still ached to think about it. But, even though she was sad about the wedding, and the end of all the things she'd envisioned for their lives together, she didn't find Christopher crossing her mind very often.

Sometimes she found herself feeling sad about the breakup, or angry about the way he had gone about it, but oddly she didn't find herself thinking about Christopher *himself.* She certainly didn't find herself constantly distracted by thoughts of him. Not the way she was by thoughts of Jack.

Jack's main goal, in most relationships, was always to avoid getting too close. As someone who had been overshadowed by his family and their prestigious medical careers for much of his life, it was important to Jack to be his own person. But avoiding closeness was difficult in the tiny quarantined room. It had only been a few hours, and he already wasn't sure he would be able to make it for that much longer.

At first their sharing a room had seemed practical. But now that Jack was faced with the fact that he would be sleeping just a few feet from Kat that very night… He tried to make certain his behavior was as gentlemanlike as possible at all times. If he couldn't hide his attraction from himself, then he at least wanted to hide it from her.

Kat sat meditating on her gurney. She seemed so serene. She was ambitious, just as Sophie had been, but then, he could never picture Sophie practicing at a hospital like Oahu General, focusing on patient care rather than prestigious research projects.

Kat certainly wasn't like Sophie. Usually when people in the medical world learned who Jack's family was they couldn't wait to talk to him about how his father's books had changed their lives, or how his mother had inspired them to go into medicine. But in six weeks Kat hadn't said a thing to him, despite knowing.

Except for just a moment ago, when she'd simply mentioned his parents' books and he'd assumed the worst. He wondered now if he'd acted prematurely.

Kat was obviously at the top of her field. She should be at a prestigious hospital on the mainland. Somewhere far away from him. Then he wouldn't have to think about the red curls cascading down her back. What was she doing here, on his island, at *his* hospital?

With all those books she looked as if she should be going on some sort of meditation retreat.

When he stepped over to the carefully organized set of workbooks that were piled in a neat stack at the edge of Kat's gurney she yanked her headphones out.

"Sorry if I interrupted," he said.

"I wasn't having much success anyway," she said. "It's kind of hard to focus on the present moment when you're stuck in a small room with bad lighting, waiting to find out if you've contracted a life-threatening illness."

He nodded in agreement and picked up one of the books. "'*Zen and the Art of You,*'" he read aloud. "'*Finding the Inner Child Within Your Inner Self.*' What *is* all this stuff?"

"It's part of my project to learn how to relax," said Kat. "I thought I'd use this time to get into my Zen."

"Into your... Zen?"

She tried to explain. "It's like...trying to live in the moment. To take life one step at a time. Not to plan, but to accept what comes in each moment."

"To go with the flow?"

"Exactly," said Kat. "Only, it's harder than it sounds. Especially since I've never been a very go-with-the-flow type of person."

He raised his eyebrows in mock surprise. "You're kidding?"

She glared at him, and he briefly considered whether he might need to duck and run for cover.

But then she groaned and said, "Look, this stuff doesn't come naturally to me. I've never been very good at letting go of all the things I have to worry about. When I lived in Chicago, sometimes I tried going to the beach on Lake Michigan to de-stress—but you know what happened every time? I couldn't shut my brain off. I'd think about the patients who needed me, or the things I'd left unfinished, or other doctors and nurses I needed to communicate with. Or the hundred other things I had to do the next day. It was so hard to figure out how to let it all go that eventually I stopped trying."

"But you're trying again now? What changed?"

Her face grew sad. "The Day of Doom," she said.

That sounded pretty intense. Was that the reason Kat had wanted to move to Hawaii? He'd simply assumed that she wanted a break from her regular life, or had romantic illusions about working in a tropical setting. It had never occurred to him that she might be running away from something.

"I suppose it does sound dramatic," she continued.

For a moment he thought she might be blinking back tears, but it must simply be the way the light hit her eyes.

"It was just a bad breakup, really. That and some other things all happened at once. Just bad timing."

Ah. So she wasn't running from something so much as some*one*. "Breakups are hard," he said. "If it makes you feel any better you're not the only one who's ever run off to Hawaii after a bad breakup."

She lifted her eyebrows. "You?"

"Me. After my own exceptionally hard breakup."

She gave a soft chuckle. "So we're both unlucky in love? And I thought you and I had nothing in common."

He snorted. "I'd have to believe in love first, in order for us to have that in common."

"Oh, no, you don't," she said.

"Don't what?"

"Don't try to beat me at cynicism. My breakup was way worse than yours—I guarantee it. No one believes in love less than I do. Trust me, pal, I have given up on love."

He raised his eyebrows. "Have you?"

"What—you don't believe me?"

"You just don't seem to be the type to give up on love."

"Oh, but I have. I've given up on love way harder than you ever could."

"Wait a minute," he said. "Has this become a contest, Kat? Are we having a contest to see which of us believes in love the least?"

She laughed. "Yes. We're having a contest to see who is the saddest and unluckiest in love, because that might be the only way to cheer ourselves up. So tell me if you can top this: my fiancé left me just three days before our wedding."

"Hmm…" he mused. "That *is* going to be hard to beat. But I think I can."

"I don't know… I think when it comes to sad love stories, getting jilted three days before your wedding is going to win every time."

"How about this? My fiancée left me for my brother."

Jack didn't know why he was telling her this. He never talked about Sophie with anyone. But talking to Kat felt so easy.

She stopped laughing and grew quiet.

"It's all right," he said. "It was a long time ago."

"What happened to her?"

"She lives in Nebraska now. She's a doctor too."

He wasn't sure he was ready for this after all. He flipped the pages of one of Kat's workbooks, which seemed to contain very specific instructions on how to achieve a relaxed state.

"You know, I'm not sure you're doing this right," he said.

"Excuse me?" she said. "Is there a *wrong* way to relax?"

"I'm just not sure relaxing is something you can learn from a book," he said. "I mean, doesn't it seem like what you're doing is the exact opposite of what you're trying to learn?"

She bristled. "What are you talking about?"

He picked up the color-coded document that Kat had printed out, which outlined each major school of thought on meditation and Kat's views on their various pros and cons.

"You're meant to be trying to learn how to live in the moment, but you're doing it exactly the way you've always done things: by planning, organizing, and obsessively studying everything there is to know about relaxing. You're practically getting yourself another doctorate in relaxation."

She snatched the document from him. "That may be the case, but this is the only way I've ever been able to learn anything. I got though medical school by throwing myself at my books and studying longer and harder than anyone else."

"Yeah, but you're not in medical school anymore. You're trying to enjoy life—not study it."

"Then what do *you* think I should do, if

you're so certain all my workbooks aren't going to help?"

He considered for a moment. "So much of your life is about taking care of other people," he said. "You need some excitement that's focused on *you*, not someone else. You need something that gives you a thrill."

"A thrill?" She looked doubtful. "That goes against everything I'm reading here. All the exercises in these books are about slowing down and focusing on the present moment."

"Nothing gets you focused on the present like an adrenaline rush."

He warmed to his theme. Every time he jumped out of a helicopter to reach a patient in a remote or inaccessible area, every time he resuscitated a patient from cardiac arrest, or delivered a baby on the way to the hospital, he was completely caught up in the present moment.

"Think about it," he said. "When do you feel the most calm, the most confident?"

"Hmm…" she said slowly. "Probably those moments in the ER when we're slammed with trauma cases."

"Exactly," said Jack. "It's the same for me. You get totally lost in the moment. You forget about any of your own worries and problems and just focus on what's in front of you."

"Okay," she said thoughtfully. "You might be

on to something. But I can't just spend my entire life in the ER. That kind of defeats the purpose of learning how to relax when I'm not at work."

He shook his head. "You don't have to spend your life in the ER."

"Then what?"

"It could be anything," he said. "Something that feeds your sense of adventure. Something new...something exciting. Something crazy and out of the box. Hiking, surfing, cliff jumping..."

"Cliff jumping?"

"Hurtling yourself off a cliff into the ocean is a great way to gain mental clarity. You're never as certain of what you want in your life as you are when you're falling through the air."

"Um...because you're facing death?"

"Facing death? Absolutely not." Then, before he could stop himself, "I'll take you. We'll only jump in places where I know exactly how deep the water is and what the rocks are like underneath. Safety first. Safety is what makes it exciting instead of terrifying."

Wait a minute. You're supposed to be trying to spend less time with her—not more. The second this quarantine is lifted you're out of here, remember? Whether that's ten hours or ten days from now.

But she was already smiling back at him. "Spoken like a true paramedic," she said.

At the sight of her smile he could feel his resolve to keep his distance slipping away. He needed to regroup.

"Well," he said, "when we get out of here maybe a group of us can go. The two of us and Marceline, Kimo…"

He saw something change in her eyes. Was it disappointment? Or relief?

"Sure," she said. "What better way to bond than over dangerous, death-defying stunts?"

"Not dangerous—*exciting*," he said. "I wouldn't let anything happen to you."

She gave him another small smile, making her face glow. "I'm starting to believe that's true. But, since the two of us are stuck in here for now, would you happen to have any ideas about what kind of exciting thrills we could enjoy in a five-hundred-square-foot, poorly lit, windowless room?"

Jack didn't dare voice the first suggestion that came to mind. Or the second. Or the third.

Instead, he simply said, "I play a mean Gin Rummy, if that's the kind of thrill you have in mind?"

A few hour later Kat lay on her gurney, trying unsuccessfully to sleep.

She kept replaying that conversation with Jack in her head. For one moment she'd almost thought he was suggesting they go on a date. But that was stupid. What had he ever done that would even remotely have given her that impression?

He'd simply meant to help her as a friend. He'd been watching her try to relax and he'd actually come up with a pretty good idea. How had she never thought of it before? Jack had been absolutely right to notice that she felt the most like herself when she was caught up in life-or-death situations. It was one reason she loved her ER shifts so much. The intensity of getting a patient's heart going again, or rushing to alleviate a trauma survivor's pain, was thrilling for her.

Cliff jumping.

As crazy as it sounded, Kat couldn't stop thinking about it. Hadn't her entire decision to come to Hawaii been one giant, impulsive leap into the unknown? After making such a huge change to her life, jumping off a cliff might almost feel easy in comparison.

It had been kind of Jack to offer to take her. Although he'd been eager to clarify that he was only suggesting they go as friends. And he'd been so adamant in asserting that she wouldn't come to any harm. He'd seemed almost fierce in his protectiveness of her.

But that was probably because he was a responsible person. He'd be protective of any friend he was with.

So why couldn't she sleep? Why was she just lying here, feeling disappointment settle into her stomach over and over again?

She thought about when he'd told her he didn't believe in love. She'd said the same to him. But did he really mean that? And what if he did? Why should it matter to her?

Suddenly Kat couldn't stand it for a moment longer. She was done with being in quarantine.

She sat straight up on her gurney and threw off her blankets.

This ends now, she thought. *I'm not staying here another minute longer than I absolutely have to.*

She had a plan, and she had no doubt that Jack would agree with it. After all, it was what a good friend would do.

Several feet away, Jack was failing to get any sleep as well. He glared at the privacy curtain that surrounded his gurney. Why the hell did it have to be so thin?

To his surprise, he saw it was rustling. And then Kat appeared in front of him.

"Hey…" Her voice was low, husky. "Can we talk for a sec?"

"What is it?" he asked as she stood in front of him in a pair of pink silk pajamas.

He didn't want to admit just how much he'd allowed this very scene to creep into his wildest fantasies—fantasies he'd been trying to push out of his mind since the moment they'd been put into quarantine together. The ridiculous idea that she'd slip into his enclosure, gaze into his eyes, and say something like...

"We need to take our clothes off."

Jack looked at her in disbelief, uncertain of how to take in what he'd just heard. "We need to *what?*" he said.

"Strip," she replied matter-of-factly. "I don't know about you, but I can't take it in here for another minute—and I'm sure as hell not spending the next ten days here. All my research with the experts from the university has indicated that patients with the super-flu virus become symptomatic within the first twelve hours of exposure. Neither of us has shown even the slightest sign of having contracted the virus. So here's what we're going to do. You'll examine me, I'll examine you, and once we've confirmed that there's absolutely no sign of the illness in either of us we'll call Selena. After all, I'm the one who's been studying this illness more than anyone on staff. I think I should be qualified to tell whether the two of us have been infected or not."

Jack noticed that Kat was shaking. Was she really so desperate to get out of here? He wondered if she was starting to get claustrophobic in the cramped space. Or maybe she just wanted to get away from him.

"If this is about needing to get some space, I'm sure we can tell Selena that we've changed our minds and want separate rooms," Jack said.

"That won't work. The hospital's at capacity. But that actually works in our favor. If we can convince her that we're showing no signs of the virus right now, it means one more free room in the hospital."

Jack considered this. Compared to the prospects of limited entertainment, uncomfortable sleeping arrangements, and hospital food, the thought of getting out of here was tempting.

The problem was, the idea of a naked Kat in front of him was pretty tempting, too.

The pajamas that Kat wore were pretty thin. He could see the curve of her hip underneath her pajama top. The silk shorts revealed long, slender legs.

He decided to try reasoning with her on a professional level.

"If this is about you being afraid of having contracted the flu, I wouldn't worry too much," he said. "The chances are extremely low. They've just got us quarantined in here out of an abundance of precaution. I know it's a hassle, but it's the appropriate procedure to follow."

"It's not that," said Kat. "I doubt either one of us actually has the flu. I just have to get out of here."

Jack was trying to muster his better self. In all the ways he had pictured the two of them together—and despite himself, despite every rational thought, he *had* been picturing it—he had never imagined it like this: him and Kat quarantined together in an isolated hospital room, surrounded by medical supplies.

To make matters worse, her request meant that she clearly thought of him as nothing more than a friend. She'd never ask such a thing of him if she had the slightest inkling of his feelings for her—or if she had any feelings for him.

He made a last weak attempt to do the right thing. "Wouldn't you rather wait until morning?" he said. "The blood test results might not take much longer—maybe the infectious disease team will have some good news for us by then."

"I can't wait until morning," said Kat. "I can't wait another minute."

She hastily began to unbutton her pajama top.

It was too much for Jack.

"Hold on," he said, putting his hands over hers. He could feel her trembling, just as she had been in the water when they'd first met. "Are you sure this is what you want?"

She gritted her teeth and grabbed his T-shirt. "Jack. We are getting out of here. *Tonight.*"

There was no arguing with the determination in her voice. Or her eyes. Jack had a feeling that no one crossed Kat when she was in this kind of mood.

The authority in her voice was intimidating. Her eyes burned into him.

He took a deep breath. His only hope was to remain as professional as possible. He didn't know how he was going to handle seeing Kat naked. He had been trying so hard to avoid thinking about her body…and now it was going to appear right in front of him. Only not in the way he'd fantasized about. The only way he was going to get through this was by putting as much professional distance between himself and Kat as possible.

"All right," he said. "If we're going to do this, we're going to be professional about it."

"Agreed," she replied. "Let's get the lights on."

Jack flipped a switch and harsh fluorescent lighting flooded the room.

Perfect. The least romantic lighting possible

in one of the most sterile rooms imaginable. This is about as unsexy as it gets, and that's exactly how it needs to be right now.

He pulled a coin from the nightstand next to his gurney. "Flip to see who gets examined first?" he said.

"Don't bother. I'll go first," she said.

I hope you know what you're doing, Kat thought to herself.

She was certain that if she could prove that neither she nor Jack were showing any sign of the virus then she'd be able to convince Selena to let them leave this room. Then she wouldn't have to deal with this tantalizing closeness any more.

It had seemed like a great idea just a few minutes ago.

Now, in the harsh reality of the fluorescent overhead lighting, she was having second thoughts.

But she and Jack were both medical professionals. Surely they could be professional about this? They'd do a thorough examination of one another and then they'd be able to go home. As a doctor, Kat had long ago set aside any sense of squeamishness about undergoing or conducting examinations. This was simply what needed to be done—for the sake of her well-being and Jack's.

She couldn't stand waiting for the blood test results for another minute. She was at her absolute limit. She needed to get away from Jack as soon as possible. Seeing him naked might be a bit overwhelming, but only for a few moments. She could withstand a few moments of being close to him if it meant that she would be on her way home after it was over.

Her fingers shook so much that she kept fumbling the buttons of her pajama top.

"Here," he said. "Let me help."

He briskly undid the remaining silk buttons of her top, one by one. The top fell open, revealing the inner curves of her breasts. She kept her eyes locked with Jack's as he slipped the top from her shoulders and it fell to the floor with the quiet rustle of crumpling silk.

He cleared his throat and then, in a clipped, professional voice, said, "Let's start from the top."

Jack cupped her face, palpating her jawline.

"I'll need you to come a little closer so I can see your scalp," he said.

She stepped forward, only inches away from him. She couldn't stop herself from breathing in deeply. This close, his scent was intoxicating. She could barely stand. But Jack was pulling her inward, looking through her hair for any sign of the flu rash on the skin of her scalp and the back of her neck.

She tried to remain perfectly still. She didn't want to make the situation any more uncomfortable than it had to be. She was the one who'd asked for this, she reminded herself. And she was probably the last person that Jack was interested in seeing naked. He was doing her a favor. The least she could do was be professional about it.

After a few moments Jack stepped away from her. "Everything up top looks good," he said. "Let's take a look at the rest of you."

Was it just her imagination or had his voice seemed to break just a little at the end? Was he nervous? Kat couldn't think why he would be. He'd made it clear that at the very most he was only interested in her friendship. Examining her naked body was probably, for him, just the same as it would be when he examined any other patient.

He placed both his hands on her shoulders and ran them down her arms, feeling for any inconsistencies in her skin. Then he turned her around and ran his hands lightly over her back. His hands felt rough—rough enough to have a texture, but not too much. She could tell he used them often, both for hard work and as sensitive instruments. They were hands that could rescue a drowning swimmer or pound a heart back to life.

Her own heart was pounding pretty hard. She couldn't help but give a small shiver.

"Sorry," he said, instantly attentive. "Are you cold?"

"N-no. I'm fine," she managed to stammer.

His hands moved faster now. Over her back and arms, rubbing her skin as though he were trying to warm her up. He turned Kat's body so that she was facing him again, and brought one of his hands up to touch her breast.

But before going on he stopped, his hand in midair. Their eyes locked.

Suddenly Kat knew that what she wanted had nothing to do with a professional examination. And it had nothing to do with any remote worry that she might have contracted the virus.

She stood in front of Jack, vulnerable, exposed, and she didn't know what to do next. She reached for him, ready to tell him that this whole idea was a mistake and that he didn't have to continue with the examination. She stepped an inch closer to him, reaching for the hand that still hovered over her breast.

Before she knew what had happened she found herself enveloped in Jack's arms. His mouth was covering hers, and she was kissing him back just as passionately. The scent of sun and salt water overtook her senses. His strong arms held her close to him, and then she was fumbling to reach under the soft gray T-shirt he slept in, which chafed enticingly against her bare breasts.

They broke for a moment as she lifted the shirt over his head, and then he kissed her again, and she lost herself in the feeling of her skin against his, his arms circling her.

He hoisted her onto the gurney and then climbed in himself. She lifted her hips so he could slide her pajama bottoms down and then off. A voice in her head cried out that *this* was what she had wanted—had, in fact, been looking for since he'd rescued her. There was no logic to it. There was only feeling: a solid, steady feeling that *this* was what she needed, *this* was the feeling she had been craving. *This* was living in the moment.

There had been no planning, no agonizing over the right decision, no making a pro versus con list and calculating her next step. She was completely caught up in the sensation of *Jack*— the roughness of his palms against her shoulders, her breasts; the strength of his chest and arms, the sweet-salt taste of his mouth crushed against her own.

Suddenly, they both froze. Someone was knocking on the door of the quarantine room.

"Kat?" Selena's voice rang out. "Jack? Is it okay if I come in?"

They leapt away from one another.

"Just give us a second!" Kat called out.

Kat stuffed her legs into her pajama bottoms at a furious pace. She tried to fasten the buttons on her top, but kept matching the buttons with the wrong hole. Finally she gave up and settled for wrapping the top around herself and folding her arms tightly in front of her, hoping Selena wouldn't see anything amiss.

Jack threw his shirt over his head and nodded at Kat. "C'mon in," he called to Selena, once he and Kat had perched themselves casually on a gurney, looking for all the world as though they'd been enjoying a casual midnight game of cards.

Selena entered the room and took in the scene: rumpled sheets, and a breathless Kat and Jack sitting next to each other on the same gurney.

"Sorry to visit you two so late at night, but I thought you'd want to hear right away," she said. "We've had a false alarm. The patient did not have the virus. It was just an ordinary case of shingles, which both of you will have been vaccinated against. So there's no need for either of you to be in here any longer."

"That's great!" said Kat and Jack, both at once.

"I had a feeling you'd be glad to hear it," Selena said. "I'm sure you're both eager to get out of here."

"Can't wait," said Kat.

"Neither can I," said Jack. "I'm not sure either of us could have handled one more minute stuck in here."

"Glad to be the bearer of good news," said Selena, turning to leave. "Oh, by the way, Jack, your shirt is on inside out."

CHAPTER FIVE

KAT FLOPPED HERSELF onto the sofa in Selena's office and let out a groan of frustration. A week had passed since the night she and Jack had been quarantined together. They hadn't seen much of each other since then, but when their paths had crossed they'd been friendly, polite, and professional with one another. There had been absolutely no discussion of their heated moment in the quarantine room.

As far as Kat could tell Jack seemed to want to pretend it had never happened. And if that was what he wanted, then she was happy to oblige.

Or so she told herself.

She might be able to stop herself from talking about that moment, but she couldn't stop herself from thinking about it. The way his hands had felt on her back, her shoulders, her thighs. The way his scent had completely enveloped her...the way his arms had enfolded her so completely.

The way he'd slipped off her pajama bottoms seconds before Selena had knocked on the door.

She was mortified by her behavior. Jack had been completely cool and clinical while he examined her—until she'd thrown herself at him like some sort of sex-crazed maniac. Her cheeks burned at the memory. He'd been trying to maintain a professional atmosphere. *She* had been the one to completely misinterpret the situation.

It was true that as their kiss had continued he'd seemed just as caught up in the moment as she had been. He hadn't objected when she'd removed his shirt, hadn't hesitated to assist her in the removal of the rest of her own clothing. But that only meant that he'd been swept away by the moment—a moment *she'd* instigated. His actions didn't mean that he'd shared the same feelings she'd had.

Kat agonized over what might have happened if Selena hadn't made her appearance.

In that moment her whole body had been crying out for Jack.

How far would they have gone?

Would having sex with Jack have cleared away all that tension, or added to it?

Kat realized that all those questions simply

left her head spinning. Once again she was over-analyzing everything—trying to solve her situation with Jack like a puzzle, rather than focusing on what was right in front of her.

And what *was* in front of her?

A pile of evidence indicating that, at best, she and Jack were friends and nothing more. Two people shut up with one another for any period of time with nothing to do were bound to get confused into thinking they were developing feelings for one another.

But Jack didn't have any feelings for her that Kat could discern. She'd been practically naked in his hands and he'd been calm and collected, focusing on his examination of her skin. *She* was the one who had thrown herself at him. She hadn't been able to help herself. The sensation of his hands on her skin, of her bare breasts against his chest, still left her feeling a little dizzy.

Fortunately she was already slumped on Selena's couch, so dizziness wouldn't be a problem.

She'd wanted to keep the details of her time in quarantine with Jack a secret, but it ached to come bursting out of her. She was desperate for someone to understand, and Selena was one of her oldest friends.

Still, unburdening herself would probably be a lot easier if Selena's eyes weren't glowing with so much excitement over the rim of her coffee cup.

"I knew I should have found you separate rooms."

Despite her words, Kat caught Selena's wry smile as she sipped her coffee.

"This is serious, Selena," said Kat. "I don't know what to do."

"Why do you have to *do* anything?" asked Selena sensibly. "It sounds to me as though you like him. And, from what you describe, it sounds like he's into you as well. Didn't you say he asked you out on a date?"

"Not a *date* date. Not at all. Just a group thing...with friends."

Selena made a face of disgust. "'Group thing?' What a cop-out. If he likes you, why doesn't he just ask you out?"

"I'm not so sure he *does* like me," said Kat. "That kiss could have meant anything. For all I know it was completely one-sided. He was a perfect gentleman when I asked him to examine me. He was completely professional about it. I was the one who made it awkward by practically throwing myself into his arms."

Selena rolled her eyes. "Even if you *were* the one who started things, it sounds as though he was pretty willing to go along with it. Maybe... and I know this is a crazy idea, but hear me out…just maybe, the two of you might try *talking to each other* about how you feel."

"Oh, God," said Kat. "That's what I was afraid you were going to say. Selena, I can't bring this up with him. I just can't. What if he doesn't feel the same way?"

"Now, there's a good place to start. You say you're worried he may not feel the same way… but, Kat, do you even know how you feel about Jack?"

Kat paused and thought for a moment. How *did* she feel about Jack?

"I guess…after Christopher… I thought I was ready to swear off relationships… Not forever, but for a long time. I don't even know if I believe there's such a thing as love anymore."

Selena's eyes bored into Kat's skull. "Kat, I don't believe that you don't believe in love. I've known you for years, and that's just not you. But I *do* believe that you've been hurt, and that you're afraid of what could happen if you let yourself get involved with someone again."

Kat sighed. "I wish there was some way to test the waters without the chance that either of us could get hurt."

"Well, I guess you could just renounce love, cover your heart in armor, and never feel anything for anyone again. But that's just not you."

No, it wasn't. Selena knew her well. She was

lucky to have such a wise friend who could offer her sage, sensible advice in times of need.

"Then again," Selena continued, with a gleam in her eye, "maybe there *is* a way you can find what you're looking for without either of you getting hurt."

Kat looked at Selena warily. "What are you suggesting?"

"I'm suggesting that if your feelings for Jack are purely on a physical level—if you truly don't think either of you are ready for a relationship of any kind—then why don't you just deal with those feelings?"

"Oh, come on, Selena!" said Kat. "Are you suggesting I just walk up to him and suggest that we…we just…?"

Selena raised her eyebrows. "Start doing the dirty deed? The hibbety-dibbety?"

Kat choked on her coffee. "Those are quite the colorful terms," she sputtered. "And even if I were going to act on it, I wouldn't know where to start. I don't even know if he's interested in me. Not in *that* way. If he was, wouldn't he be seeking me out? We barely talk to one another."

"You haven't been seeking *him* out, either," said Selena.

What if it was that simple?

What if Jack was just as eager as she was

to finish what they'd started in quarantine, but didn't know how to approach her?

He couldn't possibly have any *romantic* feelings for her, but what if he was at least physically attracted to her?

They'd both said that neither of them believed in love…but what if there was a way to take emotion out of the equation?

She thought again of Jack's suggestion that she needed a thrill. Well, there was more than one way to seek excitement…

An idea began to form in her mind. It was risky, of course. But the only potential negative consequence was that she might feel embarrassed. And since she'd already embarrassed herself as much as she possibly could in front of Jack, one more moment of humiliation wasn't going to make much of a difference.

All she had to do was find him and pop the question.

Jack was having a hard time staying focused.

He was in one of the hospital supply closets, gathering up various medical supplies to restock the ambulance's med kit, but he was finding it impossible to keep his mind on his work.

He kept taking the wrong items, or looking down and finding that he'd put too much of something in his box. Jack scowled at himself. He'd completely lost count of what he'd taken. Inventory was going to be pissed.

It had been like this for the past few days. He was able to focus just fine during emergency jobs. Just like always, when he was in the middle of an emergency he was at his peak performance. There was something about getting caught up completely in the moment and focusing on a medical emergency that allowed him to re-center himself, no matter what kind of emotional turmoil he might be going through.

But during the quieter times…when his mind had time to wander…it wandered straight back to Kat.

And specifically to that kiss.

He was completely mortified by his lack of professionalism. He'd been struggling to maintain a detached, clinical demeanor, and he'd utterly failed. Kat had been vulnerable and afraid and he'd taken advantage of her vulnerability. He couldn't have felt worse.

But he also couldn't keep his mind from returning to the way his hand had fit perfectly around her hip. To the softness of her skin. The way her hair had tickled his face when he'd buried his nose in it and inhaled the faintly tropical scent that wafted from her.

To make matters even worse, not only had he failed to hold himself to his professional standards...he'd *liked* kissing Kat. He'd felt... *desire*.

The plain fact was, he wanted more of Kat. And, try as he might to deny it, he knew deep down that he wasn't going to stop thinking about her. His body burned to finish what they'd started.

But would Kat even want to talk to him after he'd let himself get so carried away? They'd known each other for a little over a month, and this was already the second time he'd been unprofessional with her in a medical setting.

And yet during their kiss he'd felt her hands clutching at him, sensed her body pressing against his. In the heat of that moment she had wanted him, too.

But did she still want him? Or had her reaction to him simply been a response to a tense, pressured moment? In either case, he didn't know what to do.

More than anything, he wished he could call Matt. Even if his brother couldn't solve the problem, he would at least listen and understand.

But for the past four years that he and Matt hadn't been speaking Jack had had to work through his emotional problems on his own.

He had lost his wingman and his confidant—the person he'd relied on most when it had come to figuring out his feelings.

His solution had been simply to avoid deep relationships, even non-romantic ones, and all the troublesome emotions that went along with them. But now that Kat was in the picture he wasn't sure how well that strategy would work.

He had tried to give Kat plenty of space since their time in quarantine had ended. He didn't want her to feel that he expected any more of her than she wanted to give. If she was interested in him, then she could make the next move. But he wouldn't blame Kat if she never wanted to see him again.

Which was why he was completely surprised when he turned around with his supply box and saw her standing in front of him.

"Sorry," she said. "Didn't mean to startle you."

She walked up to Jack and took the box from him, setting it on the floor.

"Well, this takes me back," she said. "It's been a couple weeks since we were in such close quarters together."

Was she angry at him?

Her face bore the same resolute look, the same determined set of her lips, that he'd noticed while they'd been in quarantine. Whatever she wanted to talk to him about, he realized there was no avoiding it. Not when she looked like that.

"I've been thinking," she said. "We're both adults. And we've gotten to know each other quickly, in a pretty short amount of time, due to circumstances beyond our control. But, no matter how unusual those circumstances may have been, they don't change the fact that we're in this situation now."

"And…what exactly *is* our situation?"

She took a deep breath. "I've been thinking a lot about that moment in quarantine."

He waited without breathing. He thought his heart might have stopped.

She went on. "You know the moment I mean. When we…kissed."

Her eyes flickered straight to his and he knew his heart hadn't stopped after all. It was pounding jackhammer-hard.

"I don't know about you," she said, "but I've had a hard time *not* thinking about it. The kiss, I mean. And I know you said that you don't believe in relationships. Neither do I. But in a way that makes us kind of ideal for one another right now."

He wondered where this was going. "How so?" he said.

"Well," she continued, looking nervous, but

clearly determined to carry her point through, "anything involving emotions would probably be a terrible idea—for both of us. But then I started thinking that not every relationship has to involve emotions. Some relationships have a more…physical basis."

He was suddenly very aware that without the supply box in his arms there was nothing between the two of them. He would barely have to reach out to slip an arm around her waist. Her nose was inches from his. It was very hard to think clearly with her standing so close.

"Emotions are complicated," he agreed, his voice growing husky. "Are you suggesting that we try letting things get more…physical between us?"

She nodded, gazing up into his eyes. He noticed that the top of her head would fit perfectly underneath his chin if she were just a few inches closer.

"I was thinking that, since we seem to have some physical feelings for each other, we could deal with those feelings on a physical level. But no deeper emotions. No romance."

It was exactly what he wanted—so why did he feel a surge of disappointment? Hadn't he been trying to avoid his physical attraction to Kat precisely because he didn't want to toy with her emotions or awaken any of his own?

He needed to be clear with her about who he was, to make sure she didn't get hurt. "I don't do hearts and flowers," he said.

"Who the hell said anything about hearts and flowers?" she replied.

"I just want to be clear about who I am. And what you're looking for."

"I know exactly what I'm looking for. Look, I was engaged to someone I thought I loved. He did the whole hearts and flowers thing. I've had enough of them. I've had enough of thinking about the future, the long term, the happily-ever-after. I want something different. You said when we were in quarantine that you don't believe in love. Well, neither do I. Love's not what I'm looking for right now. If I were, I'd be looking somewhere else."

"Are you sure this is what you want?" he said.

Despite the dim light in the supply closet he thought he could see a wicked gleam in Kat's eye.

"You were the one who said I needed a thrill," she said. "I'm trying to learn to live in the moment. And you did say you would help…"

"As long as we're clear about our expectations from the beginning."

"Crystal-clear," she said.

Kat pressed close against him. Any fleeting

resistance, any reasons not to get involved that he might have briefly entertained were fading away.

And then his lips were brushing hers before he even knew what had happened. She was kissing him back, more deeply, and his tongue explored her mouth, desiring every inch of her that she could give. Her lips crushed against his, and he felt himself become swept away with the taste of her.

He wasn't sure how much time passed before she broke their kiss, pulling her head away from his. She still leaned against him, and his arms remained around her waist. As she looked up into his eyes he thought he saw flecks of gold within the green.

"So," she said, "I take it that we're in agreement? A purely physical relationship, to address an attraction that's on a purely physical level?"

"If you're in, I'm in," he said. "Purely physical. No emotions, no strings attached."

She let out a breath, as though she'd been holding it. "We should probably set up some ground rules," she said, suddenly seeming nervous. "Maybe we should make a list of what we expect from one another, to make sure things don't get too emotional…"

He pulled her closer to him again. "Here's the only ground rule I want to work out right now," he said, his voice husky. "My place or yours?"

* * *

The next night found Kat laying out three different outfits on her bed, repeatedly accepting and rejecting each one.

It didn't matter what she wore, she tried to tell herself. She and Jack weren't supposed to be trying to impress each other. She didn't need to care if he liked what she wore. And yet somehow tonight it was unusually difficult to make an outfit choice.

The more she thought about her arrangement with Jack, the more confident she became that it was a brilliant idea. She'd only had a few boyfriends in her life, and all the way up until Christopher she'd been a serial monogamist, going through one long-term relationship at a time. Part of her was still a bit shocked at her proposal to Jack—but mostly she was excited about her first foray into spontaneous thrill-seeking. She was nervous, but excited, and she intended to enjoy every minute of it.

Even though it would be her first time having sex since before the breakup…

It's just a meaningless fling, she reminded herself. *Don't put too much pressure on it.*

Over the two years she'd dated Christopher she'd tried to meet his expectations in every way possible. He was a career-driven perfectionist, and she'd thought she'd admired those qualities in him. She'd even thought that she and Christopher were a little bit similar in that way.

But Christopher's perfectionism had always seemed to involve making her feel *less*, somehow. Every time he'd told her that she'd look great if she worked out a little more, or that her hair would look nice if she'd only wear it in a certain way, she'd believed him, and tried to do what would make him happy. But it had never seemed to be enough. And in the end it hadn't been.

Her arrangement with Jack meant that neither of them had to worry about expectations. The thought of that was wonderfully freeing. Tonight would be her first serious attempt to let loose and let go.

Kat's heart pounded in her chest as she pulled into the driveway of Jack's house on the beach. She wrapped her black leather trench coat more tightly around herself as she stepped out of the car. Her outfit was a risk; she was wearing the trench coat, heels, and not much else. She'd been a little worried about what might happen if she got pulled over, but she'd been very careful to drive at exactly the speed limit for the entire drive to Jack's house.

The nice thing about keeping their relationship on a physical level, she thought, was that now she could freely admit her attraction to Jack without worrying about where it might lead. It would lead to sex with Jack and no further. Nice and simple. No other complications to worry about. No reason to be nervous.

Two hours is an awfully long time to spend deciding what to wear when you're supposedly just interested in a purely physical relationship, a small, disloyal corner of her mind piped up as she stepped out of the car.

She considered leaving her purse inside the car, underneath the passenger seat, but then she remembered the pack of condoms she'd brought with her, color-coded by type. Would Jack have thought about protection? Probably, but you never knew... Better to be on the safe side.

She grabbed her bag and walked up the sand-covered sidewalk.

He opened the door and stood in front of her, in dark jeans and a very tight white T-shirt. The T-shirt left very little to the imagination. Even in the dim porchlight she could see the firmness of his torso underneath the shirt.

And as she looked at the well-defined muscles all traces of the worry she'd had about the wisdom of her decision melted away. Whatever happened after tonight, it was going to be worth it if it gave her a chance to feel those arms pressing her against that chest one more time. This was going to be *good*.

He stood in the doorway, leaning on one arm, and she could see him taking her in. He was looking at how tightly she had her black trench coat wrapped around herself. He raised an eyebrow rakishly, taking in her bare legs, and she had a feeling that he was drawing the obvious conclusion about what else she might be wearing under the coat.

She saw him swallow, and suddenly she felt much more confident. Whatever false bravado he might display, she could tell that Jack wanted this every bit as much as she did.

She might have thrown herself at him at the hospital, but that had been then. Right now he was looking at her as though she were a package he couldn't wait to unwrap. Or a meal he'd like to devour.

She gave a shiver that had nothing to do with the cool breeze coming from the beach.

He smiled and reached down to grab one end of the belt of her trench coat, using it to pull her forward until she was pressed against him. He slipped an arm around her and pressed her closer, nuzzling his nose into her hair.

"You really came dressed for the occasion," he said, reaching down and putting his palm against her bare thigh. He murmured the words into her hair, his lips brushing against her neck as he spoke.

Her cheek was pressed against his chest, and her nose came just to the small hollow in his neck. Kat inhaled deeply. Ah, there it was… Eau de Jack Harper. She could finally allow herself to revel in it.

It was nice to be enveloped by Jack's scent without having to try to force her mind off it. But they were still outside. There was only so much that could be accomplished.

Kat marshaled her thoughts enough to say, "You have no idea. But if you want to see the rest of this outfit you're going to have to invite me in."

As she lifted her face from his chest he bent to kiss her. He still held her in his arms, though, and as he turned back into the house, he took her with him, so that they were just inside the entrance when he shut the door. He continued to kiss her, pressing her against the wall. His kisses were soft at first, then deeper and more deliberate.

Kat was grateful for the support of the wall behind her—it kept her from melting into Jack's arms right away. Her senses were full of nothing but him. But then she heard a faint ringing sound from further within the house.

Jack stopped kissing her and said, "Oh, right…the bouillabaisse. I set the timer."

"Bouley-*what*?"

"Bouillabaisse. It's French; it's a kind of stew with seafood and herbs. It's very good."

He headed further back into the house, presumably toward the kitchen, and Kat followed. Her mind was swirling. *Jack had cooked for her?* Why? She'd thought they were just going to have sex. Having a meal together...a meal he'd *cooked* for her...didn't quite fit with her idea of an emotionless night of physical passion. But then, maybe it wasn't a big deal. Plenty of people liked to cook. It didn't mean anything special.

Jack was shutting off the timer as she entered the kitchen and he grabbed a spoon. "Here, have a taste," he said, turning the heat on the stove to a low simmer and holding the spoon to Kat's lips.

Her eyes widened as she tasted the broth. "Wow, that's really good!" she said. "I don't know what I'm more excited about: eating that delicious stew, or...or..." She blushed. "Or some of our other plans for this evening."

He set down the spoon and put his hands against her hips. "Speaking of which," he said, "we were in the middle of something before that timer so rudely interrupted us..."

He leaned in and brushed her lips against his.

"Should we have dinner first?" she whispered. "I didn't know you were going to go to all this trouble."

"Actually, I'm more of a dessert-first kind of guy," he said, flicking off the stove and giving her his full attention.

Kat felt her thoughts slowly melting away as his body pressed against hers and their lips came together. And as they kissed her need for him began to intensify. The pent-up frustration of their interrupted moments had been building for days, and finally—finally—there was nothing between the two of them.

Well, not much, anyway…

Jack's hands moved to the belt of her trench coat. It was tied tight, but with a good wrench in the right direction the coat fell open, revealing her black lace underwear and nothing else.

"Wow," Jack said. "That is *not* what I expected to see under there."

"Hmm… Well, I have a few button-up blouses in my closet at home. Maybe I should wear one of those next time?" she said.

"Don't you dare," he replied, pulling her roughly to him.

He slipped the coat from her shoulders, then began kissing her neck and breasts. He lifted one breast from the cup of her bra and she gasped as his tongue circled her nipple. An arc of pleasure shot through her as he attended to one breast with his mouth while he teased and stroked the other. Then he slipped his hands under her buttocks, and she instinctively wrapped her legs around his waist as he lifted her and took them both to his bed.

She could feel the tantalizing hardness forming under his jeans...could feel that her own body was eager for him.

He tossed her onto the bed and Kat sighed with pleasure as he slid her underwear from her. She waited for him to get onto the bed with her, but instead he simply looked at her, drinking her in with his eyes. Then he knelt down by the side of the bed and pulled her forward by her hips, dragging her to the edge. He kissed the inside of one thigh, and then the other, and suddenly she realized what he was about to do.

"You—you don't have to do that," she stammered. "I mean, I've never asked anyone to... and no one's ever wanted to..."

"Then don't you think it's about time someone did?" he said.

And after that Kat couldn't speak any more, because he was placing his mouth on the hot, warm space between her legs where she felt the most ready for him to be. His tongue attended to the small nub he found there until Kat thought she would burst with the heat and the wanting. She began to cry out, but he was relentless—he was going to make her explode. And explode she did, unable to control herself against the onslaught of his mouth against her.

Kat let herself sink into the mattress, shaking. She'd wanted him, and she'd known he was ready for her, but she hadn't expected this welcome detour.

She worried that after the intensity of the pleasure she'd just felt she wouldn't have the energy to move from where she lay, rendered immobile by the sensations that washed over her, lasting and lasting. But then she saw Jack taking off his shirt, and the sight of his washboard torso gave her renewed energy.

The faint line of hair that trailed from his chest to his stomach and disappeared into his navel suggested tantalizing possibilities. She reached out for his waistband and pulled herself to a sitting position. Fumbling with the button at his waist, she pulled his jeans and boxers off in one smooth motion, revealing his firm, erect manhood.

Something clamored for attention in a small, forgotten corner of her mind. *Oh, right—protection*. But her purse was all the way out in the living room. For the briefest of seconds she despaired at the thought of having to interrupt this moment by running out to rummage through her purse. But before she could mention it Jack reached down for his jeans, where they lay on the floor, and took a condom from one of the pockets.

Kat felt gratified that she hadn't been the only one planning for their safety—and she was especially glad that having a condom close at hand meant they wouldn't have to leave the bed right now.

He eased onto the bed with her, his body firm and warm between her legs. The length of him was hard, but velvety to her touch. He locked his gaze with hers and she nodded to let him know that she was ready. He entered her in one long thrust. She lifted her hips, pressing them against his so she could let him into her as completely as possible. Their bodies joined in a timeless dance, responding to the heat and desire each felt in the other.

It felt as if it had been ages since she had made love. And lovemaking had never felt like *this*. His rhythm matched hers perfectly, his long, slow strokes mirroring the rise and fall of her body as if they were meant to fit together.

She lost all awareness of herself as sensation overtook her. She was lost in the smell of him, in the feeling of his hands on her hips and the backs of her thighs as he pushed himself into her. She ran her hands through his dark hair, as she'd wanted to since the moment she'd first laid eyes on him, arching her back. His chest was hard and warm against her breasts.

There was no sound but that of their ragged breaths melding together. Nothing existed outside of the sublime feelings that promised bliss was only moments away. She rocked her hips against his more quickly, unable to withstand the craving any longer, and his strokes came faster, pushing her toward euphoria.

She cried out in ecstasy as she felt herself shatter. And as she did, she felt him tremble within her, heard him say her name. As she raised her lips to meet his once more, she felt a tightness somewhere deep within her loosen.

They lay entangled in one another's arms, her head resting against his chest. She felt wonderfully free. There were no pressures, no tasks to accomplish. *This* moment was the moment she wanted to live in, and nothing could take her out of it.

CHAPTER SIX

JACK WOKE FIRST, to an unfamiliar whirring noise. Kat's cell phone was buzzing on the nightstand next to her side of the bed.

He gazed at Kat, who still slept peacefully, her back curved against his chest. It had been a long time since any woman had spent the night with him, but she had dropped off soon after their second round of lovemaking and he soon after.

He caressed the soft red waves of her hair, which spilled over the white pillow. The early-morning sunlight dappled her face, filtered by the tall palm trees just outside the window. She looked so peaceful.

When Kat was awake he could always read the worry in her face. She was so preoccupied with caring. No one could speak to Kat for five minutes without realizing that she was constantly thinking about everyone else: her patients, her co-workers, her friends…

Jack wondered if now he might have made it onto the list of people in Kat's life that she worried about. Cared about. And he wondered how Kat felt about the night before.

She'd seemed satisfied, but they hadn't really had the opportunity to discuss it. He was grateful that they'd put their arrangement to keep things purely physical in place. Kat might deserve more, but he knew he wasn't the one who could offer it to her.

But, if nothing else, he could offer her a good breakfast.

He'd been thrilled to find that she liked his cooking. After they'd made love the first time they'd eaten the bouillabaisse with crusty French bread. He'd loved watching her eyes widen as she'd tasted her first sip of broth, and her exclamation later, when she'd tried his homemade rosemary and strawberry ice cream.

Then, after the ice cream, they'd gotten back to the reason they'd agreed to meet in the first place. He'd loved watching her other reactions as well: her eyes drinking in his body, resting on his manhood, her breath catching as he eased his length into her.

Yes, that had been nice. More than nice.

Now, he resisted the urge to kiss the nape of her neck. He leaned over to silence Kat's cell phone and then slipped out of bed, pushing back the thick white down comforter. The heavy blanket was probably overkill in the Hawaiian heat, but he liked to be warm in bed—and it seemed she did, too.

He wondered if it was a Midwestern thing. Both he and Kat were originally from places with cold, severe winters. There'd been some winters in Nebraska when he'd feel the cold in his bones. Maybe after coming from a place like that you could never get warm enough.

He went into the kitchen and surveyed the items in his refrigerator. He wanted to make something that would let him show off a little bit, but that would also look as though he hadn't gone to too much trouble. He pulled the ingredients for crepes from the refrigerator and the pantry, setting out blackberries, strawberries, and blueberries for toppings.

He'd loved to cook ever since he was young. His parents had thought it a waste of time—why learn to cook when you could hire someone to do it for you?—but Matt had always been supportive of his hobby.

For just a moment he thought again that it would be nice to be able to call Matt, to tell him about Kat. He shrugged off the wave of sadness that always came over him whenever his brother came to mind, and tried to focus on the pleasant view of the palm trees just outside his kitchen. It was a beautiful day, as so many Hawaiian days were. They could have breakfast out on the lanai.

He wondered if Kat would want to talk about last night when she woke up. Try as he might to turn his mind to the crepes he was preparing, he couldn't get his mind off what she might be thinking...how she might be thinking of him.

As a paramedic, Jack required a certain amount of daring. He was used to running toward dangerous situations—not away from them He had to take risks every day. But for some reason those risks seemed a hell of a lot easier than talking to Kat about her feelings.

Kat woke up in Jack's bed, blinking against the morning sun. At first she was dismayed to find herself alone, but then she noticed the noises and smells from the kitchen.

Surely Jack wasn't making breakfast?

She snuggled deeper under the covers, savoring the delicious memory of the night before. Then she frowned. The plan had been for her to arrive at Jack's place, have some brisk, efficient sex, and then return home.

But nothing had gone according to plan.

Instead, everything about last night had been a sensory feast: the taste of the food he'd made for her, the feeling of their bodies intertwined, the tenderness of his gaze matching the softness of his bed.

She'd never imagined that he would cook her dinner. She'd been expecting a purely physical interaction, as they'd agreed: just sex and nothing more. But Jack had made it feel like a date. And the food had been so delicious it had almost felt as though he was trying to impress her. But why would he care about doing that?

She shivered underneath the warm comforter, remembering the feeling of Jack's skin next to hers and his hands exploring the curves of her body. Remembering his attention to her, the sensations he'd created, teasing her until her body sang with pleasure. A girl could get used to that kind of thing.

She'd meant to leave immediately afterward, but she hadn't been prepared to feel so utterly replete. She and Jack had lain in bed for some time after that first time, each of them basking in the pleasant glow that had radiated from the other's body.

She could have stayed like that forever, but then Jack had heard her stomach rumble. He'd wanted her to stay for dinner, and she hadn't felt she could leave without eating when he'd gone to so much trouble. And then they'd had ice cream afterward…and he'd kissed some of the ice cream off of her nose…and she'd returned his kiss more ardently than either of them had expected…

And then they'd returned to his big bed. And if the first time had been an expression of fierce need, the second time had been a slow and tender discovery of each other. Afterward, she'd fallen asleep without a second thought. But she'd never expected that she would wake up in his bed the next morning, listening to the clamor of pots and pans clashing together in the kitchen while he made breakfast for the two of them.

At least, she assumed it was for the two of them. Jack probably wasn't going to make something for himself and wave her out of his home.

Mission accomplished, Kat thought.

Her goal had been to let loose, and she had accomplished exactly that. All according to plan. Their "no emotions" agreement was working out just fine. Barely two months in Hawaii, and she was starting to get the hang of spontaneous thrills.

She shivered again, remembering the feeling of Jack's strong arms enveloping her, his hot skin next to hers. She could hear him humming in the kitchen. Whatever he was cooking in there, it smelled amazing. That clinched it. She was getting up.

She slipped out of bed, grabbed her phone and stumbled into the kitchen.

"Crepes okay?" Jack asked when he noticed her standing in the doorway.

She felt a surge of excitement upon learning that breakfast was indeed for both of them, although she tried to quash it down.

No emotions, remember? He's just being polite.

"I'm getting seriously spoiled with all this French food," she said.

For a moment he looked worried. "Do you like French food?" he asked. "I can always make something different if this isn't what you're in the mood for."

Kat lifted an eyebrow. She hoped it made her look like Marlene Dietrich, but she worried it made her look like a librarian giving a scolding.

She hurriedly let the eyebrow down, and said, "I'd hoped last night was enough of an indication of exactly what I like."

He seemed pleased.

Her phone whirred and she resisted the urge to check it, pushing it far away from her on the kitchen counter so that she wouldn't be tempted to look at it again.

"Do you need to get that?" said Jack.

"It's work. But we've both got the day off," she replied. "Whatever it is can wait until later, because I've decided that this morning is all about living in the moment. And *this* moment is all about crepes."

She popped a berry into her mouth, enjoying the sensation of sweetness as it burst over her tongue.

"Well, look at you, all relaxed and devil-may-care," said Jack, flipping the crepes in the pan. "Who *is* this woman who's so carefree all of a sudden?"

She shrugged and smiled. "I guess I finally found my Zen."

He spun more batter into the pan. "How does your Zen feel about crepes?"

"My Zen is very much in favor of delicious breakfast foods. And I'm so glad I get a chance to try more of your cooking. I wanted to last night, but I...we...kind of got caught up in some other things."

He smirked. "'Other things,' huh?"

She smiled and said, "You know...like the hibbety-dibbety."

"The hibbety-*what*? I don't think it's been called that since the Roaring Twenties. I think my great-grandparents might have used that one."

She blushed. "It's a private joke. A colorful euphemism Selena came up with a few days ago."

"You two seem pretty close?"

"Oh, yes, she's one of my best friends," said Kat. "We talk about everything with each other."

"Everything, huh?"

"Oh—well, now that you mention it... Maybe we should talk about how you and I are going to talk about the..."

"The hibbety-dibbety?"

She laughed. "Yes, that. What if people at work find out about us?"

"Well, we should probably take care to make sure that they don't."

For a moment she felt hurt, but then she reminded herself that Jack was just being practical. Their relationship wasn't really a relationship.

"Yes, broadcasting this around work would probably complicate things," she said.

"Exactly what I was thinking," he said. "Besides, since we've agreed to keep feelings out of it...well, it's not as though there's really anything to tell."

She lifted the coffee cup he'd given her. "Here's to not believing in love."

"Cheers," he said, clinking his own coffee cup against hers.

They were sticking to the plan. *Good.* Absolutely nothing had changed from the moment she had smelled the crepes from his bedroom

to the moment they'd sat down to have breakfast together.

The Hawaiian sun beamed onto Jack's lanai
just as brightly as ever, but if nothing had
changed, why did she suddenly feel so...

Her thoughts were interrupted by her phone,
which was whirring again.

"I've got a ton of messages from work," she
said. "They want me to come in right away."

Jack looked at his own phone. "Looks like
they want me as well. The hospital's facing a
huge surge in patients, and they want the paramedics helping out in the ER with triage and
first-line care."

"So much for our day off," Kat said. "It must
be a major emergency if they want us both to
come in. Are you ready to see how well we can
keep our secret?"

Jack left first and arrived at the hospital several minutes before Kat. The ER was inundated
with patients, all of whom were presenting with
symptoms of the super-flu.

He joined a group of doctors and nurses at
the reception desk, where Selena was briefing
the staff on the situation.

"This is my worst fear," she said. "There's
been an outbreak of the super-flu on the west-
ward side of the island, and now people are

coming here with flu symptoms." She paused and nodded at Kat, who had just arrived. "The good news is that thanks to Kat's great work with the infectious disease team, we were able to develop a vaccine ahead of the outbreak. All hospital staff have been vaccinated by now, which should increase the safety for everyone tremendously."

"We'll need to triage," said Kat. "Patients with no symptoms go to one wing of the hospital, where we can administer vaccines. Everyone showing symptoms goes to another wing, and from there we can determine level of care."

Selena nodded. "I want some of our more experienced paramedics staying in the ER today. Let's leave the ambulance callouts to the Emergency Medical Technicians. The patients who are going to need the highest levels of care are most likely already here at the hospital."

"It's all hands on deck," Selena finished. "Grab a patient, grab a chart, and get going."

Jack spent the rest of the morning caught up in the flow of ER triage. He administered vaccines to patients without flu symptoms, and sent those with more severe medical needs to the appropriate department.

He'd been working so hard that he wasn't even sure how long he'd been at the hospital when a woman pulled at his arm and begged him to take a look at her teenage son.

It was the first case Jack had seen that morning that caused him serious concern. The boy's mother said his name was Michael, and reported that he'd had a high fever and vomiting since the day before. Jack leaned in to examine Michael's cheeks, which were ashen. His face was contorted in pain, and he was holding his hand to his lower abdomen on the right side.

With a sinking feeling, Jack realized the boy probably had appendicitis. He'd need a doctor to confirm it, but based on the boy's pallor and the pain that seemed to be coming from the vicinity of his belly button, his guess was that if the appendix hadn't burst already, it would soon. Even as Jack examined the boy, he could see that his breathing was labored, and he seemed to be moving in and out of consciousness.

Michael would need surgery, fast… And Jack knew for a fact that it would be at least an hour before any of the hospital's surgeons would be free.

Jack waved at Christine, one of the nurses who was also helping with triage. "We need a gurney over here," he said. To the boy's mother, he added, "Don't be afraid. I'm going to come back with one of our doctors, and we'll do the best we can for him."

Jack straightened up. He looked out over the sea of patients that filled the ER and spotted Kat at the far end of the hall.

"Kat!" he yelled, waving to flag her down. "We've got a problem."

"What is it?" she said.

"There's a kid in the ER with what's probably appendicitis. Looks like he could be close to peritonitis."

"So call for a surgical consult."

"I will—but I already know that Ernest is out sick, and Jacquelyn's already working on a patient with a coronary artery bypass. Omar's on call, but he's at a continuing education conference across the island. Bottom line: it'll be at least an hour before a surgeon can get to this kid, and I'm not sure he can wait that long."

They'd already begun walking back toward the boy. Two nurses had already wheeled a gurney toward Michael and were easing him onto it while his mother stood by, looking worried.

"He's fading fast," said Christine quietly. "We should bag him now, because we'll need to intubate the second we get him into the OR."

Jack could see that Christine was right—Michael's breathing was so shallow as to be almost nonexistent. She had already positioned a bag-valve mask over the boy's nose and mouth. The self-inflating bag attached to the mask could be compressed to deliver oxygen to Michael's lungs until he was put on a ventilator and prepped for surgery, which needed to happen soon. Jack nodded and used both hands to apply slow, steady compressions to the bag.

"I already put in the surgical call, but it's going to be a while," Christine said. "We're going to need to make some quick decisions."

Kat's lips were a thin line. "I did a year on surgical service before I switched to internal medicine," she said.

"So you've done appendectomies before?" said Jack.

"I have, but it's been years," Kat replied.

"You might be the kid's best shot," added Jack. "Think you can do this?"

Kat paused.

She looked at Jack and Christine.

It was her call.

A year ago she might have refused. Not because she couldn't do the procedure, but because regardless of her training it wasn't her place, as an internal medicine doctor, to do surgery. But now she looked at her team and realized she had their full support.

Christine was awaiting her decision; Jack seemed confident in her.

If they could be confident, then so could she.

She'd worked long enough at Oahu General by now to know that its team could handle anything.

"Okay," she said. "Let's get him into the OR. Worst-case scenario: we keep him alive until a surgeon gets here." She yelled across the ER floor to the reception desk: "Kimo! Call Tom from Anesthesiology and tell him we're prepping a patient in OR Two. And stick your head into OR One and make sure Jacquelyn knows what we're doing, in case she closes early."

They wheeled the gurney down the hall to the OR, with Jack continuing to apply compressions to the bag-valve mask, keeping pace with the team. Michael's mother ran after. "Can I come in during the surgery?" she asked.

"Not during the surgery, but you can wait right outside," Jack said. "And I'll be out right away to let you know how things are going."

"Please," she said, "stay with him. I'll feel better if I know someone's in there looking out for him."

"Don't worry," Jack said. "Your son's in good hands."

Kat knew how Michael's mother felt, though. Jack had a way with patients that made his presence inherently reassuring. She'd felt it herself. In a crisis situation, he emanated a steady calm. She'd seen patients draw from it, no matter how much distress they were in, and she'd felt herself draw from it, too. As Kat and her team scrubbed in, while the patient was prepped for surgery, Tom, the anesthesiologist, poked his head into the scrub room.

"Just wanted to let you know that his fever spiked even higher just before we put him under," he said. "My guess is the appendix ruptured."

"Then it's a good thing we're almost ready to go in," she said.

With the patient intubated, there was no longer any reason for Jack to stay, but Kat stopped him before he left to return to the ER.

"Wait," she said. "His mother asked you to stay with him."

"Don't worry," he said, nodding toward the surgical nurses. "You're in good hands, too." But Kat thought he must have seen the fear in her eyes above her surgical mask, because after a moment's hesitation, he said, "But I'll stay to observe, if you think it's a good idea."

Kat hadn't had much chance to see the surgical nurses at Oahu General in action, but it was clear that they were experienced and knew each other well. They bantered with an ease Kat didn't feel as she began her first incision.

Her hand didn't shake, but she felt nervous. It had been several years since she'd done this procedure. Still, there was no question that the boy would die without immediate intervention. As Kat continued with the procedure her confidence grew. It took less than a minute for her to locate the appendix. As soon as she had it isolated from the other organs, she asked the nurse to place the Babcock clamps at its base.

Kat eased her scalpel along the appendix, removing it from tip to base. A cheer went up among Jack and the nurses as the appendix was removed, and Kat smiled. This atmosphere was so informal compared to what she was used to—and yet a cheer and a moment to enjoy a successful surgery seemed so appropriate to her now.

She began to close, making careful stitches on the patient's abdomen.

"Nice work," said a voice behind her. She looked over in surprise, to see Omar watching her with an appraising eye.

"Omar?" she said. "When did you get here?"

He must have driven at breakneck speed to get to the hospital from his conference.

"You were about halfway through the procedure when I got in. But you were doing so well I thought I'd just let you continue. No reason to interrupt a great job. Maybe we should get you on the surgical rotation?"

"No, thanks," she said. "Consider me a one-time pinch-hitter."

"Well, you did a great job," Omar said. "That patient is lucky you were here today. We all are."

Kat looked across the patient at Jack. She didn't know if she would have been able to do the appendectomy without him, but she was certain the procedure had been made much easier thanks to his quiet confidence pulling her through it.

Jack leaned over to look at the stitches she was finishing. "Nicely done," he said.

"See?" she replied. "I told you I was good at stitches."

It had been an exhausting day. After hours of conducting triage, administering medication and vaccines, and performing a surgery she hadn't undertaken for several years, Kat was spending the last moments of the day on the hospital's roof. She'd learned it was an excellent place to take in the Hawaiian sunrise.

She was usually alone up there, but today Jack had followed her. "You did great today," he said.

"Great?" She snorted. "You must have seen how clumsily I made that McBurney incision.

You must have seen how nervous I was. It's been years since I did any surgery."

"You saved a boy's life," he replied. "Try to focus on the big picture."

She gave a dark laugh. "I've never been very good at that," she said. "Why focus on the big picture when there are a thousand small details I can obsess over?"

"I know it's not always easy for you to stay in the moment, but this is a good one," he said. "I'm not saying the little things don't matter— I'm just saying enjoy the good you did."

"I'm trying to," she said, watching the sky change from gold to rose as the sun went down. "But it's never come easily to me. My family aren't all doctors, like yours. It was my father's dream for me to become a doctor, and after he died my mom had to work two jobs to help me get through medical school. It's important for me to be the best doctor I can be. Not just for myself, but for them, too."

He nodded. "But maybe sometimes you forget that you don't have to try to be the best anymore. You got there. You fulfilled your dreams and theirs. Now you can just be who you are."

"Be who you are?" she repeated. "It sounds so simple. But it's not." She turned toward him. "Do you know why I really came to Hawaii? I got fired, Jack. From my job at Chicago Grace."

"Why?"

"I had this whole plan I wanted to implement. This huge, sweeping plan. And I still believe in it. But I didn't bother to see if it was a good fit for that hospital. I just tried to push it through. The result was a complete disaster. And the worst part was that I felt as though I'd completely let my father down by losing my job. I didn't just want to be a good doctor there, I wanted to make a real difference in medicine... Only, once I got fired I wasn't on the superstar track anymore. And he'd always seen me as a superstar. So it wasn't just the firing that hurt... it was the feeling that I wasn't good enough."

"Maybe they weren't good enough for you?"

"The best research hospital in the country?"

"Yes. Maybe they weren't good enough for you." He put his hands on her shoulders, turned her to face him. "Kat, I know something about walking away from a path that everyone else *thinks* you should want so you can pursue what you *actually* want. It never makes sense to other people. But if it makes sense to you, then that's all that matters."

"It must have been hard for you to grow up in such a famous family with such high expectations," Kat said.

"You have no idea," Jack replied. "The only person I was ever really close to was my brother

Matt. As far as our parents were concerned, our hobbies were going to school and doing our homework. Anything non-academic was out of the question. And then, when I did try medical school, I could never trust any of the students or professors to be real with me. No one wanted to get to know *me*. They just wanted to know what it was like to be one of *the* Harpers."

"For me it was different," she said. "My family is poor, and I'm the only one who's ever gone to medical school. I felt like I had to prove to everyone that I was good enough. And then I met Christopher, who I thought was perfect. But the more I think about what happened between us, the more I think that he may have thought he was perfect too. So I had to prove to Christopher that I could keep up, that I was good enough."

"Like I said before—maybe he wasn't good enough for you."

Kat gave this some thought. It felt different to think about other people living up to *her* expectations for a change.

"Whatever happened back in Chicago, I'm sure your father would have understood," Jack said. "I know you well enough by now to know that if you believed in something enough to get fired over it, then it must have been important. Being fired doesn't matter. Being the version of yourself that you want to be is what matters."

The version of herself that she wanted to be.

The question came at her again. Who *was* she? Not anyone's fiancée, not a superstar... But today, as she sat on the hospital rooftop watching the sun go down, she felt as if she was exactly what she had always wanted to be: a doctor.

She slipped her arm through Jack's and wondered if, amidst all the chaos and crises of the day, she might have found a little bit of inner peace.

As Kat's first few weeks began to turn into her first few months at Oahu General Hospital, she thought that she and Jack were maintaining the guise of being in a purely professional relationship fairly well. No one seemed to suspect anything.

Selena had given Kat a few knowing looks, but had stopped after Kat had assured her with a deadpan expression that there was nothing worth discussing between herself and Jack.

It wasn't even a lie, Kat thought. She'd said there was nothing worth discussing—not that there was nothing happening. And, since she didn't want to discuss her trysts with Jack at all, her statement was technically true. Besides, Selena herself had suggested that Kat needed a "fling." If this—whatever it was she was hav-

ing with Jack—was just a fling, then there was
no need to discuss it with anyone.

She didn't think that she and Jack were acting any differently at work. He handed off cases
to her as they came in, giving her brief, professional summaries of the patients. They nodded
to each other whenever they passed in the hall,
and included each other in collegial conversa-
tions.

They also slipped into the supply closet in
the hospital's rarely used west wing at every
opportunity.

As far as Kat could tell, no one seemed to notice how frequently Jack needed to stock up on
painkillers just moments after she happened to
slip in to the closet to check on the availability
of gauze.

The supply closet was the perfect place for
their meetings, because it was the furthest from
the ER and therefore the most rarely used. This
meant that not only were they unlikely to be
interrupted, but that there was plenty of empty
shelf space for Kat to lean against as Jack kissed
her. He was a few inches taller than her, and it
helped to have a clear space where she could let
her shoulders lean as she lifted her head to reach
his, and where he could wrap his arms around
her without fear of knocking anything over.

His nose nuzzled into her collar now, as he

peppered her neck with tiny kisses. "Don't…
you have…a meeting…to get to?" he queried,
between each kiss.

"Not until later," she said, arching her back
to press herself into him, pressing her mouth to
his so she could explore every nook.

He twined his arms around her waist, holding
her close to him, breathing in deeply as though
he could inhale her very essence.

Usually, they were able to make the most of
the little time they had together. But Jack's mention of the meeting brought Kat back to earth
with a crash. She'd been trying not to think
about it, but now that he'd mentioned it she
couldn't get it out of her mind.

She'd hoped he wouldn't notice her distrac-
tion, but as usual he noticed everything. "What's
wrong?" he said.

"It's nothing. It's just…" They'd said no emotions, but she needed someone she could talk
to. "I could really use some advice," she said.
"Selena's great, but she's such a close friend that
I worry she wouldn't be honest with me, because she'd be so afraid of hurting my feelings.
I need some advice from someone whose opinion I respect but who doesn't…*care* about me."

She couldn't be certain in the darkness, but
she almost thought she saw him frown.

"I know we said no emotions or personal stuff," she said, quickly.

"No, it's okay," he said. "How can I help?"

"Do you think I fit in here?" she asked.

He pulled away from her, looking surprised. "Of course," he said. "Look at how well you're doing. You've helped develop a vaccine for a serious illness threatening the island. You did an appendectomy when you hadn't done one in years. How could you think you aren't fitting in?"

She sighed. "I had a meeting with the other doctors yesterday morning. We were talking about some of the policy changes I've put in place since coming here. Specifically, the one that's had the most impact on their work: the requirement that everyone spends eight hours a month working at the hospital's walk-in clinic."

There had been lots of grumbling about that—not without justification. The doctors felt it was an unfair increase to their workload, even though Kat had tried to adjust the schedules to prevent their hours from increasing.

"That's really important to you, isn't it?" Jack said. "But you're worried about a repeat of what happened at your last hospital?"

She nodded. "At Chicago Grace I tried to get them to open up a free, nonprofit clinic. We could have subsidized the extra cost with research and grant proposals. There would have been a *very* slight impact on the hospital's profits over the first three years, but that would have evened out over time."

He winced. "I bet they didn't like hearing that."

"No, they really didn't. In fact…" her face looked more worried than ever "…that's what they fired me over."

"What? *How?*"

"They wanted me to bury all my data showing that only wealthy patients improved after leaving the hospital. Those who couldn't afford follow-up care just stayed the same or got sicker. I refused."

"I can't believe they fired you for something like that."

"Maybe I should mention that when I refused I was shouting at the top of my lungs. And I may also have told the entire board of directors that they should lose their medical licenses because of their lack of compassion for poorer patients."

"Wow! Good for you."

"And I also told the hospital's administrative director that he was a money-hungry prick."

He let out a low whistle.

Kat nodded. "I know," she said. "It doesn't really sound like me, does it?"

"Actually, it sounds *exactly* like you," he said.

"I've never seen anyone more passionate about providing good patient care. I know it sucks, getting fired, but I'm glad you don't have to work with those people anymore, and I'd have thought you would be too."

"That's the thing," she said. "I thought the problem was that I was working in the wrong environment, with the wrong people. Everyone here's been wonderful—except they seem to hate my changes, too. I *know* my idea for a nonprofit clinic can work...but only if all the doctors agree to work full shifts there. And no one seems to want to do it."

"It sounds like a great idea," he said. "But did you *ask* the doctors here what they thought about it? Or did you just rush to put your ideas into place? Did you even think about asking Marceline what she wants? Or working with Omar to figure out what he thinks would help boost patient outcomes?"

"I guess I just rushed in with my own ideas," she said. "It's not that I don't care about what they want—I *do*...so much—but it's not how I'm used to doing things. Back in Chicago, the doctors and the hospital administrators held all the authority. I can't remember the last time a hospital administrator asked me what I might need instead of telling me about some new system they wanted to implement. That kind of thinking is exactly what I wanted to get away from, and instead I've just ended up recreating it here." She looked up at him. "Do you think there's any way I can fix this?"

"I *know* you can fix this," he said. "I have a feeling you can do anything. But I'll give you a tip: here in Hawaii, informality will get you further than formality. Spend some time talking to the staff about what they need. Take things slower. They'll come around once they have a chance to see how passionate you are about this and that you want what's best for them as well."

She was smiling again. "You're really good at this, Jack."

"At what?"

"Helping me figure things out. I really appreciate it. And now I *do* need to get going, so I can get ready for my meeting."

"Hold on—let's get you presentable," he said, gently smoothing her hair and tucking a few loose strands behind her ears. Then he stopped, as though a sudden thought had occurred to him. "You know, supply closets are nice..." he said.

"Yes," she agreed. "I'm developing a certain affinity for them."

"But they can be a little claustrophobic. I was wondering if you might be interested in meeting up in a non-closet, non-quarantine, non-enclosed-space-of-any-kind type of setting."

She fixed him with a steady gaze. "Jack Harper, are you asking me out on a date?"

"Yes," he said firmly. "I do believe I am."

When Kat got off work that day she was still thinking about it.

A date. A date with Jack Harper.

It wasn't consistent with their agreement for a purely physical arrangement, but maybe it wouldn't hurt to see what happened when they took their relationship outside of the bedroom. She was surprised, though, that of all the possible moments when Jack could have asked her to go on a date he'd done so after she'd explained how she'd been fired.

Christopher's reaction to the news had been quite different.

Christopher was one of the best surgeons at Chicago Grace Memorial, and Kat had always believed their relationship was storybook-perfect. While they'd been dating she'd been proud to be with someone so disciplined. Christopher had always been the one to get up for a five a.m. run. He lived off kale smoothies…ate nothing but protein and vegetables…

Kat had always felt that she fell short of living up to his regimented lifestyle. But Christopher was handsome, he was disciplined, and she had thought he loved her.

She had never thought he wouldn't support her when she was fired from Chicago Grace.

"I thought we were people who were serious about our careers," he'd said. "I thought I was about to marry the head of internal medicine at one of the best hospitals in the country. Not an idealistic fool who would throw her career away because she can't hold back from insulting the hospital's board of directors. Well, I won't be foolish with you. You can do what you like with your own reputation, but I won't let you damage mine."

He'd had more to say, but by then she'd slammed her engagement ring on the table and left.

At the time, she'd thought she was heartbroken. But now she wondered if her heartbreak was really about Christopher at all. Her sadness had more to do with having had to let go of the expectations and the life she'd thought she'd wanted. Christopher hadn't been the love of her life after all—he'd simply been a symptom of a larger problem. He'd simply fitted in perfectly with her own high expectations and perfectionism, her misguided idea that she somehow had to earn the right to be accepted.

But since setting foot in Hawaii she'd begun

to feel accepted just as she was. And the more time she spent with the people she cared about—Selena, her co-workers and, yes, Jack—the more she felt she didn't need to change herself. She only needed to *be* herself.

CHAPTER SEVEN

KAT WAS SKEPTICAL about Jack's plans for their date, but he assured her that shave ice was a beloved Hawaiian delicacy.

"You can't truly say you've been to Hawaii without trying shave ice," he said. "Personally, I think it's an absolute travesty that you've been here this long without having any."

Kat was reluctant to crush Jack's enthusiasm, but based on his description she wasn't sure she could see the appeal.

"It sounds like it's basically a snow cone," she said.

"Blasphemy," he said. "Shave ice is *nothing* like a snow cone."

"But it's essentially shaved ice covered with syrup?"

"Okay, first of all, it's *shave* ice—not *shaved*. Please try not to embarrass me when you order."

"So they shave the ice...?"

"Into a very fine, snowy powder—yes. And

then you pick the flavor of syrup you want to go over it."

"So, like I said, it's basically a snow cone."

"Not one bit," he said. "Don't let anyone hear you say that. You'll get voted off the island immediately."

She rolled her eyes and elbowed him in the ribs.

But the shave ice did turn out to be different from a snow cone. In fact, it was different from anything she'd ever eaten before. Snowy, powder-soft ice shavings were packed on top of coconut ice cream, then covered with tropical fruit syrup and a topping of condensed milk. The result was an incredibly soft, fluffy confection that made Kat think of ice-cold pudding.

"What do you think?" asked Jack.

She took another bite and closed her eyes. "It's like eating a cloud," she said, "or a fluffy milkshake."

He snorted, but she could see that he was pleased that she was enjoying the icy treat.

"A fluffy milkshake, huh?" he said. "That's one I haven't heard before."

They sat down at a colorful picnic table to eat. The shave ice stand was crowded, and Kat could see that Jack was right: shave ice was extremely popular. The lawn in front of the stand was densely packed with people.

But they had barely taken their first few bites before they heard a commotion at the far end of the lawn. Kat stared, wondering what was going on, and then she heard faint cries of, "Oh, my God! Somebody call 911!" and "Is there a doctor anywhere?"

Jack leapt into action, with Kat close behind him.

A man was slumped over his bowl of shave ice and now he slid from the picnic table. He didn't seem to have fainted, but Kat could see he was in danger of losing consciousness. He was slightly overweight, aged about forty. A woman who seemed to be his wife stood next to him and two children, a boy and a girl, stood nearby. The boy appeared to be trying not to cry; he had his arm around the girl, who looked to be about five and was crying profusely.

"He was fine just a minute ago..." The woman was distraught.

"It's okay—I'm a doctor and he's a paramedic," Kat said, and motioned toward Jack, who was checking the man's vitals as best he could without any equipment. "I need to know what happened."

"He...he said he was tired. We'd been hiking, and we missed lunch because of the hike," the woman said.

"Okay, deep breaths," said Kat. "Does he

have any medical conditions that we should know about?"

Given the suddenness of the man's fall, and the fact that he'd missed a meal, her money was on some form of hypoglycemic shock—possibly due to diabetes.

Just as she was forming that thought, Jack said, "Kat, he's on an insulin pump." He pulled at the lower half of the man's shirt to reveal the device.

The pump was common for people with Type One diabetes. Small and portable, it could be worn discreetly under most clothing. It was meant to deliver small, continuous doses of insulin to the body throughout the day, rather like a portable pancreas. But insulin pumps weren't always reliable, and the danger could be significant if a pump malfunctioned.

"Check to see it's functioning properly," Kat said.

"Doesn't look like it," Jack responded. "I can't even read the screen."

"Did he complain of any dizziness earlier today?" Kat asked the man's wife. "Any shakiness, sweating, rapid heart rate?"

"It's hard to say," the woman responded. "We've just been up Diamond Head. He was a little shaky, and sweating quite a bit, but so were the children and I. We assumed it was just the result of a long hike in the heat."

"Could just be heatstroke," said Jack. "Although the broken pump makes insulin shock more likely. Does he have a glucagon rescue kit?"

The man's wife buried her face in her hands. "He was prescribed one six months ago but we never thought we'd need it. We left it in the hotel...an hour from here."

"Call it in," said Kat, but Jack was already on his phone, talking to ambulance dispatch. "What are his vitals?" she asked him.

"Pulse is fast. He's conscious, but just barely."

"Can he swallow?"

Jack looked up to see an employee of the shave ice stand among the gathered crowd. "Can you bring us a bottle of syrup?" he said. "Any flavor. We need to get his blood sugar up *now*."

A moment later someone handed Jack a bottle of strawberry syrup and a paper cup. He poured a small amount of syrup into the cup while Kat knelt by the man's head and tried to keep him conscious.

If the man could stay conscious long enough to swallow the syrup, they'd be able to raise his blood sugar enough to revive him, so that he would simply need to be stabilized at the hospital. But if he fell unconscious there would be no way to raise his blood sugar until the ambulance arrived.

Kat knew the nearest ambulance was at least twenty minutes away, and every minute counted. Every second their patient continued to suffer from insulin shock was crucial, and she desperately wanted to prevent the man from slipping into a coma and suffering all the complications that would arise from that.

"Raise his head a little," said Jack, and Kat supported the man by his shoulders.

His wife knelt down to help her support the man's weight.

"Here, let him lean back on you while he drinks," Kat said to her.

Jack held the cup to the man's lips and tipped it back slightly. The man managed one swallow, then two.

"Easy does it," said Jack. "We just want to give the insulin something to work with, so that your blood sugar can stabilize. Right now it's way too low. The good news is that you're still awake, so you can keep swallowing this syrup."

Kat was impressed with Jack's calm tone. She'd heard him use the same one while bringing patients into the ER, and she knew firsthand how reassuring his confident tone could be. She knew that he wanted to try to normalize things for the family, to reassure the children that help was here for them and for their father. Sometimes talking helped everyone to stay calm.

Jack kept on tipping the syrup into the man's mouth, one swallow at a time, until the man was able to hold the cup himself. Kat was relieved. He was probably out of danger.

After a few more minutes the ambulance pulled up. Kat recognized two EMTs from Oahu General, who nodded at her and Jack as they took over.

"You're in good hands now," Jack said, patting the man's shoulder and giving a reassuring glance to his wife.

As Jack and Kat moved back from the patient to give the EMTs a chance to safely assist him into the ambulance, the manager of the shave ice stand appeared behind them. He was holding large-sized bowls of the same ices they'd ordered.

"On the house," he said. "I noticed you didn't get to eat yours before they melted because you were busy saving that man's life."

As they were eating, Kat said, "Jack, you really are an amazing paramedic. With skills like yours...with a family like yours...why didn't you become a doctor?"

He put down his spoon and gave her a grim look. "That question answers itself."

"I'm not sure I understand..."

He sighed. "You have no idea what it's like to be constantly noticed as one of *those* Harpers. With a family like mine you always have to wonder if people really care about *you*, or if it's just about your connections and the career advancement those connections can provide. When I was in medical school I was always wondering... Does this person want to be my friend, or do they want my dad to offer them a summer internship? Does that professor really think I did a good job on that procedure, or does he want me to mention his name to my mother?"

She thought about that. Jack was right; she didn't have any idea what that would be like. She'd been the first in her family to graduate from college, let alone go to medical school. She'd known plenty of other students who'd come to medical school already having family and other connections in the field, and she'd often been envious of those connections, but for Jack it sounded like having a family that was so well-known in the medical community was more of a liability than anything else.

"I bet there were times when it really sucked," she said. "Not only would you be constantly wondering whether people liked you for *you*, but you'd also be dealing with some pretty high expectations."

"You have no idea," he said again. "Most kids

get to dream about what they want to be when they grow up. For my brothers and me it was a foregone conclusion: we were going to be doctors, whether we wanted to or not. And everyone assumed we wanted to. My brother Matt was the only person I could really talk to about it."

"Do you get to see him much?"

"Not really. Have you always known you wanted to be a doctor?" he asked quickly.

She had a feeling he wanted to change the subject, and she was happy to oblige. She was curious about him, but she didn't want to push for more than he was ready to give.

"It's been a dream of mine ever since I was very young," Kat said. "My dad passed away when I was ten. Pneumonia. Maybe things would have been different if he'd been able to see a doctor sooner, but he was always working, and sometimes he'd put off going to the doctor to save money."

Jack nodded. "That's why the idea of opening a nonprofit clinic at Chicago Grace was so important to you? That's why you got so mad when they told you no?"

Kat gave a terse nod. "If there's any way I can make it so that fewer families have to go through what mine did, I'll do it."

"I can't imagine losing a parent at such a

young age," Jack said. "It must have changed everything?"

"Pretty much everything," she agreed. "I think that was the beginning of my Type A tendencies. I turned into a little adult. If I wasn't the one worrying about the bills our electricity would go out. I can't fault my mom, though. She might not have been the most organized person in the world, but she worked hard to put me through school."

"It doesn't sound like you had the chance to have much of a childhood."

"Yes and no. My family was poor, but I never felt poor because I felt loved. And even though I had to work pretty hard—I started working part-time jobs when I was sixteen to save up to pay for school—I still feel it was all worth it in the end." She brightened. "And it's not as though I can't make up for lost time. Maybe I didn't get the chance to do anything wild or reckless when I was younger, but opportunities continue to present themselves." She gave him a wicked smile.

"Oh? And what kind of opportunities might those be?"

"Well, I believe I recall one of us suggesting cliff jumping as a fun recreational pastime."

He laughed. "You can't be serious."

Her eyes widened innocently. "Why not?"

Truth be told, she'd been wildly curious about the idea of cliff jumping ever since he'd suggested it. And she didn't want to wait around to see if any of their friends wanted to go. She wanted to go now—with him—before she lost her nerve.

"I think you were right when you said that I needed some excitement, some kind of thrill. This is my chance. Besides, you said it was great for mental clarity."

"That's true," he said, his face growing thoughtful. "You're never more certain of what you really want than when you're hurtling through the air at top speed. Into appropriately deep water, of course." He glared down at her. "Safety first," he said sternly.

"Of course," she said. "So—are we doing this?"

"Let's go."

Jack had been driving for about an hour. They were almost to the spot of coastline that was his destination—the perfect spot for cliff jumping. Something was still bothering him, but he wasn't sure how to bring it up.

Just say it, he thought. *You're about to literally jump off a cliff with this woman. If you're not afraid of that you shouldn't be afraid of an emotional conversation.*

He summoned his courage. "Earlier...when you were telling me about how hard you had to work to get through medical school... I couldn't help but feel guilty," he said.

"Guilty? Why on earth should you feel guilty?" she asked.

"Because I walked away from something you worked so hard for," he said. "I left medical school at the end of my third year but I could have sailed through—because of who my parents are, and because my family have money. You had to scrimp and save and plan your whole life to get something that I gave up."

"It wasn't what you wanted," she said. "Becoming a doctor has always been my dream. But it doesn't sound as though it was ever yours. Why feel guilty just because you decided to walk away from the path that I chose?"

He was relieved to hear that she wasn't appalled by his decision. But Kat wasn't finished.

"There is something I wonder about, though," she said. "You said earlier that you were closest to your brother Matt, but that you don't see him much now. Why not?"

"My older brother and I haven't spoken in four years," he said.

He wasn't sure why he was opening up to her. Maybe because she'd been so sympathetic. His struggle was nothing, compared to hers, but she seemed to understand exactly what he was saying.

"Oh," said Kat. "This wouldn't happen to be the same brother you told me about while we were in quarantine? The one who cheated with your fiancée?"

"That's the one," said Jack.

He'd always refused to talk about Matt and Sophie. He'd simply decided to leave that part of his life behind. He wasn't sure why he felt he could talk about it now, except that there was something about Kat's ability to understand him that seemed to make his words come tumbling out.

"Matt was the only person in my family who I could really be myself with," said Jack. "I looked up to him."

"Sounds like you were pretty close," said Kat.

"We were. Matt was a great older brother while we were growing up. He always stood up for me, listened to me, and he helped me out whenever I needed it."

"So what happened?"

"It's complicated," he said. "When I left medical school to join the SEALs Sophie felt that I'd let her down. She was in medical school too, and she'd always planned for a certain kind of life. She wanted to be married to someone who was a doctor, like she was, and she wanted a big house in the same suburb my parents lived in. And then I didn't want those things anymore."

Kat placed a hand on his arm. "It's hard when people grow apart," she said. "But if you wanted such different things maybe it's for the best that you didn't end up together."

"I can see that now," Jack said. "But at the time I was heartbroken. It wasn't just that she didn't want to be with me. I could have understood that. She'd thought all along that I wanted one kind of life, and then I started trying to explain that I wanted something different... Even though I'd hoped she would understand, I would never have faulted her for still wanting a different life than the one I'd started looking for. If it had just been that I would have gotten over it in time."

He took a deep breath. "But then I found out that she'd been cheating on me with Matt. She left me for him the next day. I confronted Matt and told him that I couldn't believe he would do that to me."

"How could he?" said Kat. "How could your family accept that from either of them?"

He sighed, and then he said, "Sophie was pregnant."

Kat paused for a moment, and Jack's heart went cold at the shocked expression on her face.

"You have a child?" she said. But then understanding broke through. Her hand went to her mouth. "Oh, no. It wasn't yours, was it?"

He winced. "See? I told you I was naïve. *You* put it together right away." He gave a dry laugh. "Matt knew the baby was his. He and Sophie had been cheating on me for six months. I've always wondered if she viewed Matt and I as somehow interchangeable. As long as she married into the Harper family she'd have the connections she needed to work at any hospital she liked for the rest of her life."

"But that's not all, is it?" asked Kat.

"What do you mean?"

"Jack, it sounds to me like you and your brother were incredibly close. To lose that relationship, especially when you didn't have many other people you felt you could count on…it must have been devastating."

He shrugged, reluctant to let her know how right she was.

"Have you ever thought about calling him?" she asked.

"No way," he said. "I don't need the complication."

"Jack, family isn't a complication. It's *family*. You have a niece or nephew to get to know."

"No," he said. "I *thought* I had a family. Instead I have a group of people back in Nebraska who are interested in prestige and not much else, and who all happen to share the same last name."

He was taken aback by the bitterness in his own voice, and surprised when Kat said softly, "I can understand why you'd feel that way. It sounds like Sophie confirmed your worst fear: that people were only interested in you for your family's prestige and connections."

"Exactly. And then when you came, with your incredible reputation and your plans to change all the policies at the hospital…"

"You thought I was some bigwig who'd put my career over the people in my life."

He had the grace to blush. "I can see how wrong I was about that now. People come here all the time, thinking they're going to escape their problems, or they're going to jumpstart their careers by being a big fish in a small pond. But it's *my* small pond, and I'm very protective of it."

She thought for a moment, and then she said, "It might surprise you to hear this, but I know how it feels to be used for your connections."

"Oh?"

"When I got fired from Chicago Grace, Christopher called off the wedding right away. We'd both thought I was going to be promoted to director of the internal medicine department, and when I didn't get the promotion, and then got fired, he broke up with me."

Jack shook his head. This Christopher guy was a complete idiot.

"Anyway, this whole year I've been trying to figure out why I'm not grieving Christopher more. I was going to marry him. I thought he was the love of my life. But I feel like I've been more upset over losing my job than losing my fiancé. *Ex*-fiancé."

"Well, your job was something you worked hard for most of your life. Your career was about you and about your connection with your dad. Who never even met Christopher. So it makes sense that losing your job would have affected you much more deeply."

"Yes, but it's more than that. I don't think Christopher and I were really meant to be. I thought he loved me… But now I think he just loved the idea of being married to a department head at a top Chicago hospital. He liked the prestige. But when it came to really making a difference in the way I wanted to he didn't care."

Jack pulled off the highway and parked underneath a tree just beside the road. They'd reached their destination.

As they both got out of the car, he said, "It sounds like we've both broken away from our old lives. And now we can figure out what to do with our new lives—what the next steps are."

They approached the edge of the cliff at the golden hour—the hour before the sun set and cast everything with a luminous glow. It was one of Jack's favorite spots in all Hawaii: a stretch of coastline on the island's north shore. This part of the shoreline was made of high cliffs, with deep water below. It was an ideal spot for cliff jumping, if Kat decided she wanted to go through with it.

Being so close to the shoreline awed Jack, as it always did. And as he looked at Kat he could tell that she was just as taken by the island's beauty as he was.

"It's incredible," she said. "I've never seen water this shade of blue before. It's like looking at liquid lapis lazuli."

Jack realized he'd never really taken in the islands through someone else's eyes. Kat's response to the wild beauty of Oahu made him feel as though he were seeing it all again for the first time.

"You love this place," he said.

"I think I do," she replied. "Even though I haven't spent much time here. From the moment I got off the plane I felt like I was home. Chicago is a great city, but it's very...flat. I've never seen a place that radiates so much natural beauty as Hawaii."

Speaking of radiating beauty, Jack thought, *she should see how her face softens and her eyes shine when she looks out over the cliffs.*

Somewhere along their hike to the cliffs she'd plucked a plumeria flower and placed it in her hair. The effect was breathtaking now, as Kat looked out over the coast, framed by the sea and sky, her tangled red hair waving in the wind. She turned toward him and somehow, before he knew what had taken hold of him, he'd reached out and she was in his arms, her face tilted up toward his.

He felt as though she'd always belonged there—as though he'd reached out for some lost piece of himself that he hadn't known was missing. But to have her so close was confusing. He couldn't think clearly with her pulled into his arms, pressed against his chest, her hair smelling of flowers.

He found himself saying, "There's no reason to be scared," and he couldn't be sure if he was saying it to her, or to himself.

"Scared?" she said. She looked up at him, confused. "Why would I be scared?"

A fair enough question. She rested securely in his arms and he would damn well *never* let any harm come to her if he could help it. She was in the safest place she could possibly be, even if she didn't know it. So why should either of them be scared?

He searched his mind for an explanation of what he'd said—something that would make sense. "I was talking about the cliff-jumping, if you decide you want to try it," he said. "It's always scary the first time, but there's nothing to be afraid of here. The water's deep, but we're close enough to shore that we can swim back safely, and the current isn't overpowering."

She looked up at him, still folded in his arms, her eyes filled with emotion. "Jumping off a cliff doesn't scare me," she said. "I know that might sound strange. But you were right, Jack! I was never going to learn to relax from a book. I need to try new things, and I need a thrill. I'm the kind of person who relaxes by finding excitement—not by sitting in a quiet room meditating. But before coming to Hawaii I never realized that about myself because my whole life has been about studying. I never even had a chance to experience an adrenaline rush until I started working in the ER. I don't think I ever realized that *that's* what I love about medicine: the excitement, the unpredictability, having to think quickly. At least, I didn't realize it until I met you."

Jack wondered if Kat could feel his heart

beating underneath his shirt. He'd pulled her to him and she hadn't pulled away. She was still resting in his arms, her head against his chest, as though she belonged there. As though she *wanted* to be there. As though whatever was between the two of them wasn't about being friends, or having a physical relationship with no emotions.

She held him as though she wanted him.

She held him the same way he was holding her.

"I'm not scared of jumping off a cliff, Jack," she continued. "Why would I be? I trust you. But I'll tell you what I really *am* scared of." She locked her eyes with his. "I'm scared of the two of us hiding from how we really feel about each other."

And then she was kissing him, her lips seeking his with ardent desire, and he found himself kissing her back just as passionately, his tongue desperate to explore every last corner of her mouth and his arms pressing her against his body, right where she belonged.

Some time later their kisses became shorter and softer, until they simply held each other close, their foreheads pressed together.

"What do you think?" he said. "Should we take the leap?"

She looked over the cliff. "The relationship leap or the actual leap?"

"Both," he said.

"I want to, but I'm not sure I know how," she said.

He held her close. "I think there's only one way to do it," he said. "Take a running start, hold hands, and jump together."

Kat's head broke the surface of the water. She felt exhilarated. She looked around and for a moment was worried not to see Jack, but then there he was, swimming toward her.

The leaping off—pushing her legs up and out, away from the cliff—had been the most frightening part, but it had helped to have that running start. And it had also helped to know that Jack was holding her hand. They'd run for the edge together, holding hands for as long as they could before they leapt into the air and broke apart.

For an endless moment that had seemed to exist outside of time she'd hung in the air. It had been the closest thing to flying she'd ever experienced. With her feet springing away from land, the sea rushing toward her and the salt air surrounding her, her senses had been completely enveloped. There had been no room for her to fret about the past or worry about the future. The only moment she'd been able to completely exist in had been the present.

Then the water had rushed up to greet her and surrounded her body. She'd let herself sink, and then relaxed her body until it had naturally begun to rise toward the surface. She'd kicked her way up to the air, breaking the water's surface with a gasp.

And now Jack was swimming toward her with sure and steady strokes.

He'd been right. About so many things. About her need for excitement. About the two of them taking a chance on one another.

He swam toward her, wrapped his arm around her waist, and kissed her.

Jumping off the cliff had felt like a microcosm of her life, she thought. You could plan and plan, she thought, but nothing could prevent you from hitting the water in the end. The question was, did you want to fall off or jump off freely, feeling the sensation of flying?

She looked over at Jack. The future would come, and life would have its twists and turns, its bumps and bruises, no matter what she did. She'd never be able to completely avoid life's setbacks or challenges.

But she could choose who she'd be holding hands with when they came.

CHAPTER EIGHT

IN CHICAGO, IT had often been hard for Kat to face the cold gray mornings. If the sun made an appearance at all, it usually didn't show up until nine a.m., and then it was often obscured by clouds, unless the weather was exceptionally nice that day.

But mornings in Hawaii felt as though they were taking place in another world. The sun was up early, and as a result so was Kat. Her apartment wasn't far from the beach, and she enjoyed taking early-morning walks by the ocean as she sipped from a mug of coffee.

She couldn't believe how much she'd already changed during the time she'd spent in Hawaii. No one back home would ever have thought of her as a morning person. But the early hours before her shifts at the hospital were now her favorite part of the day. It was so relaxing to hear the rush of the ocean mixed with the wind and birdsong in her ears.

She smiled to herself. Just a few short months ago she hadn't known how to relax, let alone how to relax at the beach. She'd been worried she might have permanently lost her ability to live in the moment. She'd spent so long trying to build her career that she'd forgotten to focus on herself as a person.

But whatever it was she might have lost after the breakup, and everything that had happened on the Day of Doom, she'd managed to get it back. Apparently she had no trouble being spontaneous anymore. Hadn't she signed up for surfing lessons just that morning?

She couldn't wait to tell Jack. He'd mentioned that surfing was something he'd never gotten around to learning. She wondered if they might be able to learn together. Or maybe she could take the lessons on her own and then teach him. Her mind hummed with possibilities as she made her way back to her apartment.

She'd left her phone on the kitchen counter so that it wouldn't distract her from her walk— something the Old Kat never would have done. In the past she'd had to obsessively check her emails and other messages before she even got out of bed, but now she liked to savor those early moments before she started her day.

She picked up the phone. It was early, but she saw that someone had already tried to call her several times that morning. The number had a Chicago area code, though she didn't recognize it as belonging to her mother or to any of her friends.

The voicemail was fuzzy and crackly, but the important parts came through. Chicago Grace Memorial had had a major overturn in staff. There was a new hospital director, and the voicemail was from the director herself.

She said she understood that Kat's recent firing had been the result of some differences in vision between Kat and the former hospital director. But now he had been let go, along with several members of the hospital's board, so would Kat be interested in having her old job back? With an increase in pay and a promotion to Head of Internal Medicine? Chicago Grace wanted her to return very much. Could she call back as soon as possible, to let them know if she was interested?

Kat gasped. Of *course* she was interested. This was everything she'd ever wanted.

And yet somehow, she felt...flat.

She thought of all the things she'd need to do, but it was as if she were going over a laundry list. She needed to pack, to talk to Selena, to transition all her patients at Oahu General to other doctors...

Her mind went through the list mechanically.

Four months ago she would have been thrilled to get a job offer like this. But now she wasn't sure how she felt.

Without thinking, she pulled a suitcase from underneath her bed and began throwing items of clothing into it.

Wait, she thought. *You haven't even called this woman back yet. You need a timeline...you need to prepare...you need to make a checklist of all the things you have to do to get ready to go back...*

She froze. She had to go, didn't she? People didn't just turn down opportunities like this. Who knew when another chance would come along?

But if this was such a clear choice why did she feel so flat? She'd only intended to stay for a year in the first place. Selena probably wouldn't mind if she needed to negotiate a few months off her contract. Or maybe the hospital in Chicago could be convinced to let her stay the whole year in Hawaii and resume her work there after her contract was up.

There was so much to do. Should she call the hospital director back first or talk to Selena first? When should she tell Selena she was leaving?

Then her heart flipped over.

When would she tell Jack she was leaving?

And *was* she leaving?

She realized she was treating it as a foregone conclusion. But was it really what she wanted?

She paused for a moment and searched her feelings. She wanted to stay here in Hawaii. But she also missed Chicago.

She'd done the thing she'd been trying so hard *not* to do the moment she'd first laid eyes on Jack. She'd fallen for him. Leaving him was going to break her heart all over again. But it was her chance to get her career back on track.

Or was it?

Somehow, the idea of returning to Chicago Grace Memorial didn't thrill her the way she'd thought it would. She was just reacting automatically, without asking herself what she really wanted.

But what *did* she want?

She stood in her apartment, listening to the silence. Just a moment ago she had felt so happy. Now she had no idea what she wanted at all.

"So that's the situation," Kat told Selena later that morning. "They've had a change in the hospital administration and they've decided they want me back."

"I knew it was too good to be true," Selena muttered. "I get one of the top infectious disease researchers in the country to work at my hospital and of *course* she's going to leave after only four months."

"That's just it," said Kat. "I'm not so sure I want to leave."

Selena's eyebrows shot up. "How could you *not* want to leave? I mean, I love this hospital, but even *I* have to admit that it's no Chicago Grace. We're a good hospital, but Chicago has the researchers and the prestige and the funding—"

Kat cut her off. "I know it has all of those things. And I feel like I'm *supposed* to want those things… But I'm not sure that I still actually *do* want them."

"Well, if that's how you feel then it sounds like you have a lot of thinking to do— Wait a minute," Selena said abruptly. "Is there something you haven't told me?"

"Like what?" said Kat innocently.

"Like maybe the situation has deepened between you and a certain dark-haired, blue-eyed paramedic?"

For a moment Kat felt a sense of shock that Selena had clearly guessed that something was going on between herself and Jack.

Oh, what the hell? More than anything right now, you need to talk this over with a friend.

She felt a little guilty, because it was Jack's

secret as well as hers. But she needed her friend's advice.

"Jack and I have been seeing each other—" she began.

Selena squealed and said, "I *knew* it!"

"It started out as a purely physical thing. We promised not to get our emotions involved. But then, somehow... I think our emotions *did* get involved."

"And do you regret that?" asked Selena.

"The only thing I'm certain of right now is that I don't know how I feel," Kat said.

"Have you told Jack that you've been offered this new job back at your old hospital?"

"No," said Kat. "And I'm not going to. Not yet, anyway. It's a big decision, and I feel like I have to make it myself."

"Why don't you take the next few days off while you think it over?" said Selena.

"A few days off? I don't need that. And the last thing I want to do right now is take time off when I might be about to leave anyway. You asked me to come down here to help you out. I don't want to leave you in the lurch."

"Kat, we're fine. This is actually a really good time for you to take some time off. We're not facing any upcoming outbreaks right now. Thanks to the vaccine, and your initiative with the outpatient clinic, there's been a noticeable reduction in cases coming through the ER. With better access to follow-up care patients are less likely to need emergency response, because we're catching things early instead of at the last possible minute, when things are in crisis. So, largely thanks to you, we do have a moment for a breather right now."

"Time off, huh...?" said Kat. "It was bad enough when I spent just a few hours stuck in quarantine. I don't know what I'm going to do with myself if I'm not at the hospital."

Selena put her hand on Kat's shoulder. "You don't need to connect with your doctor self right now," she said. "You need to figure out what you want for *you*."

Jack stood outside, stunned by what he was hearing. Selena's office door was open just a crack. He hadn't meant to eavesdrop; he'd been coming to Selena's office to follow up on a request for some of the EMTs' time off to be approved. But he'd stopped when he'd noticed that she and Kat seemed to be having a private conversation.

Just as he'd turned away, he'd heard Selena.

"Have you told Jack that you've been offered this new job back at your old hospital?"

He'd frozen. When had that happened? How

long had Kat known? And why had she decided not to tell him?

Now, as the initial shock wore off, he realized he was still hovering outside the door. He quietly eased himself away from the entrance to Selena's office and headed into a stairwell down the hall so he could think.

It shouldn't bother him that Kat might be leaving. She'd only ever planned to stay for one year.

But she'd been on the island for…he mentally calculated the days since they'd met…a little over four months. He hadn't expected that she would leave so soon.

And if she did leave what did it matter to him? She had a life back in Chicago, and they'd both always known that she'd planned to return to it. So what if that happened much sooner than either of them had expected? They'd both agreed to have a fling. A no-strings-attached, no-expectations, no-commitment island fling.

For the rest of the afternoon he tried to avoid her as he went about his duties at the hospital. He knew he'd want to confront her if they spoke, but he didn't know why. For some reason the thought of Kat leaving seemed to have awakened something ugly in his chest—something angry and hurt and furious at the unfairness of it all. And whatever that ugly beast was he needed to hide it from Kat—because, rationally, he knew it made no sense.

He had no right to be angry. No right to confront her, to demand an explanation of what he'd overheard between her and Selena. Getting attached to one another had never been part of the plan. They'd agreed to that from the start.

But he wanted to confront her, to ask her exactly what that conversation with Selena had meant, and what she planned to do. Even though he wasn't sure if he could maintain control over his emotions.

Oahu General was a small hospital, and despite his best efforts to avoid Kat he filed a patient's chart behind the reception desk and turned to find her right in front of him.

"Supply closet. Five minutes," she whispered into his ear, and before he could respond she'd scooted away.

For a minute he considered not meeting her there. But he knew he had to. He couldn't stand not knowing if she was leaving for a moment longer.

His face stoic, he headed down to the supply closet.

Kat stood waiting for him in the darkness. She knew she should tell Jack about the job offer— she really should. But not yet. She wasn't ready.

She wanted to enjoy her time with him for just a little longer before anything else got in the way.

But when he arrived, instead of slipping quietly inside the closet as he usually did, he switched the lights on. Her stomach dropped when she saw his face. His expression was cold, even angry, she thought. And his next words confirmed her worst fear: he already knew.

"So when were you planning to tell me that you're going back to Chicago?" he said.

His voice was dull and wooden. And his eyes weren't angry, she realized. They were pained.

"How did you find out?" she asked.

"Does it matter?"

She flinched at the coldness in his voice. "For your information, I haven't decided yet whether I'll go back early or not. I did receive the offer of a job at my old hospital, with a promotion. But I made a one-year commitment to stay here, and it's important to me to honor that."

"And what happens to your job offer while you're honoring your commitment here? Are they going to wait around for you for another eight months in Chicago? I doubt it. You're going to take their offer, and you're going to take it now—because this is the kind of opportunity that a doctor like you can't stand to pass up."

"A doctor like me? What is *that* supposed to mean?"

"You know exactly what I mean. You talk a good game about healing people, but it's really all about the prestige and the glory."

She was absolutely disgusted. "I'm not your ex, Jack, and I'm not your family. Don't start confusing me with people from your past. Yes, I'm successful and ambitious, but you have no right to tell me what my priorities are."

"Is that so? You're not exactly difficult to figure out. You come to this island a big-city doc, thinking that you know better than everyone else, and then the minute something better comes along you leave. It's all about the next step—it's never about caring about where you actually *are*!"

She glared at him. "Maybe if you'd quit living in the past you wouldn't have such a hard time planning for your future!"

"*I'm* living in the past?" he said. "You've been living in the past since the moment you arrived. You just wanted a break from your normal life—you never wanted to think about how the people who live here are actual *people*. You say you want to learn to slow down and live in the moment, but the truth is you just wanted a place to recover from the *one time* someone didn't recognize your brilliance. And now that the world is ready to shower you with applause again you're going to kick the dust of Hawaii off your heels and head back to the city as soon as possible. You talk about wanting to change your life, but you haven't changed at all. You're just going right back to the life you left behind."

Kat was ready to throttle him. He was partly right—just a little bit—and that little bit was enough to set her blood boiling. But she certainly wasn't going to give him the satisfaction of letting him know that some of his words had hit home.

"At least I was able to leave it behind—even if it was only for a little while!" she said. "*You* haven't left the past behind at all. You're living in it every day."

"I am not!"

"Are you kidding me? You let your past control every single thing you do. Because you won't face any of it. You say you don't date doctors, but that's complete nonsense. You *like* doctors. You work with them every single day. You don't have a problem with doctors. You have a problem with the one you're related to. Matt. *Your brother.*"

"What happened between me and my brother is none of your business."

"Then I'll tell you something that *is* my business. Your whole no-strings-attached thing with relationships is ridiculous. It's not the real you— it's just you trying to avoid pain."

He inhaled sharply, as though she had cut him to the quick. And maybe she had gone too far. But she felt the truth of what she'd said deep within her. Jack's whole defense system—his guardedness, his pretense of being unemotional and uninterested in relationships—none of it was the *real* him, the Jack she'd gotten to know after four and a half months on the island. Even if he couldn't see it, she could—and she had to tell him, even if it hurt.

He had grown quiet, his face dark. Then he said, "If no-strings-attached is ridiculous, then where does that leave us?"

She didn't know what to say. She wished more than anything that she could have had this conversation with Jack when she was more prepared for it. After she had made her decision and had planned everything she wanted to tell him.

The silence grew. Finally, she said, "Look, Jack, this is just terrible timing. We've been having... *I've* been having a wonderful time. I thought we'd have more of it..."

His lips were a thin line. "I don't think it's terrible timing," he said. "In fact, I think it's *great* timing. Not a moment too soon."

"Please believe me when I say that I haven't made a decision yet. I'm not sure what I'm going to do. Chicago Grace is one of the best research hospitals in the country, and I can't turn that down lightly. But when I think about my time here… I don't know what to do."

"Stay, go—it doesn't matter to me," he said. "We agreed no emotions, remember? This was never supposed to be anything more than physical. So it makes no difference to me what you decide."

"It doesn't?"

"No. In fact, I think you should go."

She felt something in her chest shift and crack. She tried to look into his eyes, those blue eyes that had so captivated her the day they met, but his face was turned away from her and his eyes appeared to be fixated on a random spot on the supply closet wall.

He cleared his throat and said, "You can't turn it down. It wouldn't make any sense. You belong at a big research hospital where you can shine—not in a remote little hospital in the middle of the ocean."

"I just…" Her voice quavered and she blinked back tears.

"Congratulations on your new job," he said.

* * *

Hours later Jack was brooding on the beach—much as he had been the day he'd met Kat. He couldn't stop thinking about their argument.

"You let your past control every single thing you do," she'd said. *"Because you won't face any of it."*

What did she know about it, anyway? What business of hers was it whether he let his past control him or not? They'd agreed to keep things on a purely physical level, so why should she care about his past or how it affected him? *She* was the one who'd proposed their fling in the first place. They'd both always known that she was only here for a short time, and she knew that he didn't like getting his emotions involved in relationships.

"Your whole no-strings-attached thing with relationships is ridiculous. It's not the real you—it's just you trying to avoid pain."

It was true. In the heat of their argument he hadn't been able to bring himself to be honest with Kat, but he could be honest with himself now. She was right. He kept himself distant and guarded from women because of the pain he'd felt over Sophie. More specifically, over Sophie and Matt.

If it had been an ordinary breakup he would have gotten over it long ago, but the fact that Sophie had betrayed him with Matt meant that he'd lost the one person in the world he'd thought would always be there for him.

Strange, he thought, how he'd tried so hard to avoid repeating the pain of heartbreak and yet here it was, as fresh as ever. Even though he'd tried to convince himself that his relationship with Kat was purely physical and emotionless, it wasn't true. It really had been just his attempt to keep himself from getting hurt.

Despite his best efforts to stay distant they'd gotten close, and before he knew it he had allowed himself to hope. When they'd tried to keep their relationship purely physical their lovemaking hadn't quenched his thirst. It had only brought about a desire for more. He thought perhaps she might feel the same way, although he couldn't be sure. And now he could never ask her. As much as he was hurting right now, the last thing he wanted to do was make it harder for Kat to leave him.

You always knew she was here for just the one year, he told himself. *What were you expecting? Don't blame her just because you got your hopes up for something you knew perfectly well was never going to be long-term in the first place.*

But even though he knew it was the right thing to do, the mature thing to do, it was hard to accept the end of their relationship so soon after it had begun. He couldn't say what their time together had meant to Kat. But for him it had felt like the beginning of something. Something he wanted to explore to its fullest extent to see where it would lead.

He knew that it wasn't realistic or fair of him to hope that Kat would change her career plans for him. After all, they'd only known each other for a few months. And when he stepped back from the hurt of it all and really thought about it he knew that he would never dream of asking her. As much as he, personally, didn't believe in putting a career over personal happiness, that was *his* choice. Kat's career was the thing in her life that made her happy.

He'd never get in the way of her happiness—not for one second.

Even if that meant that they couldn't be together.

The thought of it tore at his heart.

For almost Jack's entire life there'd only been one person he'd felt cared enough about him to help him figure out situations like this. More than anything he wanted to talk to that person now. He wanted his advice, he wanted his reassurance that things would be okay, or that even if things weren't okay they'd stick together and figure it out.

He just wasn't sure he had the guts to make the call.

"You don't have a problem with doctors," Kat had said. *"You have a problem with the one you're related to. Matt. Your brother."*

His anger flared again. Was this what she'd meant when she'd said he let the past control him? As though he was too much of a coward to face his feelings?

But now his anger was more with himself than with Kat. Because right now he needed help from someone he could trust. Even if that person had made a mistake. His inability to forgive was holding him back from getting what he really needed.

Jack picked up his phone. He dialed a number that he'd deleted from his contacts but that had burned itself into his memory long ago.

He wasn't sure if he was ready for this conversation. But, ready or not, it was time for him and his brother to talk.

The phone rang once, and then Jack heard a familiar voice answer.

"Hi, Matt," he said.

CHAPTER NINE

EVER SINCE SELENA had advised her to take a
few days off, Kat had been moving nonstop.
She'd been packing, calling Selena, calling her
mother, and logging in to Oahu General's system to update her files. She'd been researching
flights to Chicago and looking up the number
of the real estate agent who'd found her apartment to see about getting out of her lease early.

She had a million things to do, and she knew,
all of a sudden, why it felt as though she had to
complete every single one of those tasks *right
now*: it was because preparing to leave helped
her to keep her mind off Jack.

As long as she kept herself busy she wouldn't
have to think about the pain in his eyes. And
she wouldn't have to dwell on that sensation of
something cracking, deep within her chest. It
was a feeling that had started as soon as she'd
looked into Jack's eyes and told him about the

job offer. She was trying, and failing, to ignore it.

She believed in love. She knew that with great certainty now. When she'd told Selena months ago that she didn't think she could believe in love or in relationships she'd been lying to herself. She'd been trying to figure out who she was and what she believed at the same time she'd been trying to mask the pain that she'd felt about Christopher. The result had been a ridiculous cynical statement that she knew now wasn't true.

There was no denying her feelings for Jack. It was true that she hadn't known him for long. She'd only been in Hawaii for a little over four months, and even less time had passed since she'd given herself permission to acknowledge her true feelings for Jack. It was too soon to know where things would go if they stayed together. And yet she felt deeply enough to know the relationship deserved a chance.

She might not know how to describe her feelings for Jack, but she knew that the only thing that held her back from using the word *love* was time. If she left now she'd spend her life wondering what might have happened if she'd stayed. Wondering if he might feel the same way.

But she had to leave, didn't she? Jack had

practically insisted she go. Chicago Grace Memorial was one of the most prestigious hospitals in the country. How could she possibly turn it down?

The answer was that she couldn't. Of course she had to go. People didn't simply turn down positions like this. Did they?

But if she wanted the job so badly why was her heart sinking? What was wrong with her? Normal people didn't react with disappointment when they were offered everything they'd ever wanted.

Taking the job would make her one of the leading infectious disease researchers in the country. She'd be able to do good, important work, and she'd be recognized as a valuable contributor to the field of medicine.

When she thought about that, she recognized herself. It felt like who she was. But she wasn't so sure she was as excited at the prospect of what daily life in Chicago had to offer. She knew that life well. Long, cold winters. Late nights spent at work. She knew she could handle that life, because she'd already done it for years. But handling day-to-day life and relishing it were two different things.

In Chicago, she knew she would earn respect from her colleagues, but would she be able to count on their friendship? Before working at

Oahu General she'd never dreamed there could be a hospital with such warm collegiality among its staff. She'd come to depend on her regular chats in Selena's office, on the casual banter among the paramedics, nurses, and physicians. These past four months had been among the happiest of her professional life.

When she thought about returning to her old life in Chicago, she had the strangest sense of dread. But surely no one in their right mind would pass up a prestigious job opportunity just because...just because they were *happier* where they were?

Before moving to Hawaii she would have known the answer to that question. Happiness could wait. She was busy building her career. She would worry about enjoying her life after she'd retired from twenty or thirty years as a respected physician. Maybe then there would be room in her life for her to make decisions based on what she wanted for herself rather than the next logical step in her career.

But since she'd moved to Hawaii she'd been able to get a taste of what it would be like to have balance in her life right *now*. She still worked hard—that was certain. But when she came to work she wasn't just passionate about her career: she had fun, too. She would genuinely miss the staff and the environment they'd created.

Leaving the hospital would be hard.

Leaving Hawaii would break her heart.

She paused in her packing to savor the cool breeze coming through the window. There truly was nowhere else on earth that was like this place. Where else would she be able to walk to the beach from her apartment and see dolphins frolicking off the coast? And she'd gotten used to the riot of color among the flowers that lined Honolulu's sidewalks. The thought of exchanging those tropical flowers for gray ice-covered walkways was disheartening.

It wasn't just that Hawaii was pretty. If it were only that her decision would be so much easier. There were plenty of pretty places in the world and she couldn't live in all of them—it wasn't physically possible. If her reluctance to leave was simply a matter of craving natural beauty, that was a problem easily solved. She could take a vacation somewhere beautiful any time she started to feel burnt out.

No, the islands were beautiful, but it wasn't their beauty that called to her. It was something deeper than that—more primal. Something she'd known in her bones the second she'd arrived. The moment she'd stepped off the plane she'd felt a sense of coming home. She couldn't remember having had such a feeling of belonging somewhere since before her father's death.

Her father had had such heady hopes and dreams for her, and by great good fortune she had shared those same hopes and dreams for herself. It had meant so much to her to live up to his expectations—especially after he'd gone. And then, as she'd grown up, it had become important to her to live up to the expectations of her teachers, her professors at medical school, her supervisors as a student and her superiors at work.

And because many of those expectations that others had had of her were also those she'd had for herself, she hadn't noticed that her own happiness was no longer a priority. Her desire for her happiness had slipped away as she'd focused on the needs and expectations of others.

So it had felt natural to live up to Christopher's expectations of her, as well. No wonder none of her friends had liked him. She hadn't been able to understand it at the time, because it had felt so natural for her to agree with Christopher and to try to please him. But she wondered now why it had never seemed as important to please herself.

But the minute she'd stepped off the plane in Hawaii she'd felt something new. That same breeze that had brought her the scent of the plumeria flowers had also brought her a sense of glorious possibility. The possibility of being herself. The mountains and the ocean had promised her adventure; the birds, the flowers and the meandering paths had hinted at peace. And the people had offered an acceptance that she'd never thought was possible.

She'd been so nervous about earning her place at Oahu General Hospital that she'd never realized she didn't *have* to earn it because her place was already there. She didn't have to work hard to belong. Instead she simply belonged.

Jack had once told her that he did his best thinking at the beach. He'd said he'd been out on the beach to think on the day they'd met, when he'd rescued her from the rip current. Kat had decided that the beach might not be a bad idea. And, thanks to Jack, she was now an expert at using the beach as a place to think, too.

Those days when she'd felt as though she couldn't turn her brain off, couldn't stop worrying about all the people who mattered to her and all the work stresses were over. The worries were still there, occasionally, but now she could set them aside and focus on the sand and the waves.

Jack had been right about her need for excitement, too. But as she strolled barefoot on the beach, feeling the sand underneath her toes, she knew that she needed the serenity that these islands could offer her as well. She wondered if she would have been able to appreciate the stillness and the calm of the ocean if Jack hadn't shown her how much she needed excitement first.

However she'd gotten to this point, she was glad that she was finally able to relax enough to enjoy something as simple as a walk on the beach. She wanted to soak up as much of Hawaii as possible. She gazed out over the ocean, marveling at its endlessness. She took in the sun, shimmering on the water's surface, and far in the distance she could see the other Hawaiian islands, where a cloudy haze formed around the green mountains of each one.

The sand was cool under her toes and for a moment Kat felt completely at peace. She was completely absorbed in the way each part of the beach touched her senses: she could feel the grains of sand that had collected on her feet, the warmth of the sun on her skin, and she could hear the sound of ocean waves in her ears, punctuated by a few birds flying overhead and calling.

She'd never felt this way about any place she'd ever been to or any choice she'd made. The closest comparison she could think of was the day she'd learned that she had gotten into medical school. In that moment she'd felt the strongest feeling of peace and security wash over her—the knowledge that she was going to do exactly what she was meant to be doing with her life.

She had that same feeling about Hawaii—that this was where she was meant to be and that she should spend the rest of her life here and continue feeling it was meant to be.

You could almost call it a kind of love, she thought. And it had been Jack who'd shown her how to fall in love with the islands, how to take advantage of all they had to offer.

I could visit, she told herself. *I could take trips to Hawaii every so often—maybe every other year or so. I could come here for holidays and long weekends.*

You don't visit the love of your life "every other year or so," her heart responded. *Not if you have any choice in the matter.*

But did she have a choice? At first, it had seemed as though she hadn't. She'd just reacted without thinking. She hadn't thought about how Jack would feel at all.

She felt a stab of pain in her chest as she remembered the hurt in his eyes. She hoped she hadn't sounded callous.

Jack had a hard time trusting anyone with his feelings. He'd grown up in a family that had put career above everything—even personal happiness.

When she'd gone through her breakup with Christopher her family and friends had rallied around her. True, she'd holed up in her apartment for several days, hiding from everyone, but once she'd been ready to face the world again she'd been inundated with supportive texts and voicemails from all the people who cared about her.

But when Jack had suffered the worst betrayal of his life he hadn't been able to go to the people he needed the most for support. That was the kind of family Jack had grown up in.

She'd gotten the impression that there hadn't been much importance placed on emotion when he was a child, and that that emotionless existence was one of the very things he'd come to Hawaii to get away from. Lonely, emotionally deprived Jack had known exactly what he needed, and he'd come here because he'd known that the islands could provide it.

And he'd known what she needed, too. He was the first person to have spoken to that wild part of her—the part that needed adventure and excitement. The part of herself that she'd gotten a glimpse of on rollercoasters and waterslides as a child…the part that she'd had to bury so deep underneath her cool, professional exterior.

A light breeze had picked up over the beach. It felt like a caress over her sun-warmed skin. She picked up a handful of sand and watched it run through her fingers. She wondered if she was doing the same thing to herself: holding happiness in her hand and letting it run through her fingers.

Jack had been able to decide that his life was about living up to his own expectations of himself. And his expectations of himself were good because he was a good person. She knew that to her core. She could see that Jack felt the same way she did about caring for the people around him—not just his patients, but everyone in his life. She and Jack might have taken different paths, but they'd gotten to the same place in the end.

Maybe her life could be about not living up to anyone's expectations but her own? Not Christopher's, not those of her family, her friends or her employers. Her father had wanted her to be a doctor, but Kat was sure that he'd wanted her to be happy, too.

But what did she want for herself?

It had been so long since she'd thought about what she wanted, rather than what everyone around her needed, that her brain felt rusty as it mulled over the question.

Jack had told her that cliff jumping was great

for mental clarity. She smiled, recalling that moment. He had certainly been right in saying that you were never more certain about what you wanted than when you were hurtling through the air. But right now she felt she needed something different.

She stood up from the warm sand. She could have stayed there all day, but it was time to move on. The sun was heating the sand to the point that it was almost too uncomfortable to sit on. Soon it would be too hot to touch.

She smiled to herself. It was as though Hawaii was telling her to get a move on. Hadn't the island always known what she needed? Even from the start, when she'd thought the island was trying to drown her, it had just been bringing her and Jack together.

It was just as Jack had said: she was never going to solve the problem of what she wanted by thinking about it. She could analyze and analyze, obsess and worry and make dozens of pro-con lists without ever figuring out the answer.

In order to work out what she wanted, she need to understand how she *felt*. And in order to know how she felt, she needed to be at peace.

Fortunately, while taking these past few days off, she'd learned a new skill that was great at offering her peace.

She'd started her surfing lessons just a few

days ago. At first it had been difficult, but she'd gotten the hang of it quickly. She'd anticipated having to learn with a bunch of tourists, but to her very great surprise, in addition to teens and adults, her introductory surfing class had included very young children—children who seemed young enough that they'd barely mastered walking, let alone surfing.

Her instructor had told her not to worry, that she'd pick it up in time, with enough practice. And then, to Kat's great surprise, the instructor's *dog* had hopped onto a surfboard of its own and paddled out with them.

No one else in the class had seemed the least bit surprised, and as Kat's lessons had progressed she started to understand why: they saw at least five other surfing dogs every morning. Apparently the dog lovers of Hawaii hated to leave their furry friends on the beach.

Determined not to be outshone by surfing dogs and babies, Kat had thrown herself into learning to surf. After all, if she was indeed leaving the islands, she'd only have so much time to learn.

She was getting better, too.

Now, she paddled her board out to the waves and sat up on it, letting the waves rock her gently. It was a pleasant way to sit and think.

She listened to the sound of the waves lapping and inhaled the salt scent of the seawater.

It was astounding, she thought, how the island seemed to have a way of knowing just what she needed. It had pushed her into Jack's arms that first day, even though she'd been so certain she didn't want a relationship. And it had pushed her toward excitement, toward new ways of challenging herself. Did the island know her better than she knew herself?

She was still thinking about that when a rogue wave knocked her from her surfboard and pushed her under the water's surface.

CHAPTER TEN

THE PHONE CONVERSATION hadn't been as difficult as Jack had expected. In some ways it had
felt like old times. And by talking to his brother
Jack felt as though an entire piece of his iden-
tity had come back.

But after several years without speaking
things were also different. Jack wasn't just
Matt's little brother anymore, forever living in
his shadow. And Jack felt that Matt respected
him in a way that he never had when the two
of them had been growing up together. He got
the distinct impression that Matt admired him
for making the phone call that he had been too
afraid to make.

"I'm not sorry that Sophie and I ended up
together, but I am sorry for how it happened,"
Matt had said. "It was unforgivable. We should
have told you as soon as it started. For my part
I kept the secret because I wanted to protect
you... I didn't want to hurt you. But I was a

coward. I should have realized that the lie would hurt you more than honesty ever would."

Jack had felt tears prick his eyes. "All that was a long time ago," he'd said.

He'd told Matt all about Kat, explaining that she was really the person who had given him the courage to make the call. If he'd never met Kat he'd probably never have tried to reconnect with Matt in the first place. And then he explained that Kat was leaving, and that he was about to lose the first person he'd been able to open his heart to in years.

At which point his brother had said something that had surprised him.

"It sounds like when she got the job offer you told her to go, to follow her career," he said. "It even sounds as though you tried to push her away."

"I didn't want her to feel as though I was trying to hold her back," Jack said. "I would never ask her to make such a major life decision based on her feelings about me. I want her to do what's best for her."

"Yeah, but who are you to decide what's best for her? Doesn't that get to be *her* decision? And wouldn't she make the best decision if she had all the information?"

"What do you mean, all the information?"

"You told her to go. But is that what you really want? I thought you said the *aloha* culture was all about being real with people? But you haven't been real with her. Why don't you tell her how you really feel about her leaving? You say you don't want to get in her way, but from everything you've said she sounds like a pretty independent woman. Don't you trust her to make the right decision for herself?"

Jack had been silent as he'd thought about this and Matt had continued.

"She can't make an informed decision if she doesn't have all the data. Maybe you think you're trying to protect her by hiding your feelings and keeping them to yourself. But if there's one thing I've learned, it's that secrets only hurt."

Jack could see the truth in that, but he was still unsure…afraid.

"What if I tell her how I feel and it doesn't matter?" he'd said. "What if she still goes back to the mainland?"

"I don't know what will happen," Matt had told him. "There's no way to know for sure. But if you tell her how you feel, with no expectations of her and no strings attached, then at least you'll know that you were honest with her and with yourself."

Honesty, Jack thought now, as he worked through his shift at the hospital. Now, there was a deceptively simple concept. Hadn't he and Kat been struggling with honesty since the moment they'd met? It had been a Herculean struggle for the two of them to be honest about their feelings with one another. And then, when they'd almost gotten there, it had all been snatched away.

Matt was right, though, Jack thought. Kat was a strong woman. She could handle the truth. And he wanted to be honest about how he felt for her. Not because he wanted to convince her to stay, but because he wanted to be real about his feelings. Kat, more than anyone else he'd ever met, had taught him that it was important to be real about what he was feeling. If she was leaving now, then he wanted her to leave knowing exactly how he felt.

Then she could use that information however she wished, without any expectations from him.

The problem was he'd been looking for her all day and hadn't been able to find her. He hadn't seen her anywhere in the ER.

It was a slow day, and there hadn't been many calls coming in that morning, but when an EMT brought in a tourist with an ankle fracture Jack offered to take the patient up to Radiology for X-rays, hoping he might see Kat there. No luck.

She wasn't in the hematology lab, nor any of the operating suites. He began popping his head into individual exam rooms, but she was nowhere to be found.

He gave up searching and went back to the reception desk, where he found Selena and Marceline.

"Is Kat coming in today?" he asked.

"She'd better," Selena said. "We're planning a surprise goodbye party for her." Then she glanced at her watch with a worried frown. "She's thirty minutes late for her shift, though. That's not like her."

Jack had stopped absorbing information after the words "surprise goodbye party."

"Wait a minute," he said. "Isn't a goodbye party a little preemptive? We don't even know if she's definitely decided to leave yet."

Selena gave him a sympathetic look. "I'd like to cling to the hope that she'll stay here too," she said. "But Kat is a talented physician. I don't think she'll turn down a job offer like this just to keep working at our little hospital." She narrowed her eyes at Jack. "Unless, of course, she has some *other reason* to stay."

Jack decided he wasn't going to rise to the bait—especially as the other half of Selena's statement had started to sink in.

"What do you mean, she's thirty minutes late for her shift?" he said.

His concern started to rise. Thirty minutes

was an eternity where Kat was concerned; she usually preferred to arrive for her shift at least twenty minutes early, so she could enjoy a cup of coffee while she prepared herself for incoming patients. Of course more recently that time had been used for their supply closet trysts... but no one needed to know that.

"You know how Kat feels about being on time for things," he said. "She wouldn't be late without a reason. Has anyone heard from her? Is anyone looking for her?"

"Now you're the one being preemptive," Selena said. "I agree that it's strange for Kat to be late for anything, but it's a little early to start worrying. For now, let's keep an eye out and assume that whatever's holding Kat up isn't too much of an emergency."

Jack didn't like it, but he knew that Selena was right. Catastrophizing wasn't going to help. But he was still worried. Kat was punctual to a fault, and he knew she wouldn't be late unless something serious had come up.

He walked by the reception desk and passed Kimo, who was preparing trays of pineapple and dried coconut for the break room.

"Hey, Jack, weren't you looking for Kat earlier?" Kimo said. "They just brought her in— in an ambulance. I think you can still catch her down there, if you hurry."

An ambulance? Oh, God. The minute he'd heard she was late he'd known something bad had to have happened.

He ran at full speed to the ambulance docking bay, where he saw a few EMTs milling about by an ambulance with open doors.

Inside he saw Kat, unconscious on a gurney.

He shoved his way through and leapt into the back of the ambulance. He started checking Kat's vitals. She appeared to be breathing— good. What had happened? Why were the EMTs acting as though nothing was wrong? Why wasn't anybody taking care of her?

"Kat?" he said. "Kat, can you hear me?"

He couldn't lose her now. His jaw set. He'd do whatever it took to fix his mistakes…assuming they could be fixed at all.

She lay in front of him, her eyes closed, her breathing shallow. Her red hair curled about her neck in ringlets and he realized that it was dripping wet—the same as it had been the day they'd first met. In fact, her whole body was soaked.

Had she met with another mishap in the ocean? If she had, he hadn't been there to leap to her rescue.

"Kat," he said again. "Please wake up."

His eyes stung and he swallowed back tears, thinking about their last conversation. Now something was wrong, and he hadn't been there, and it was his fault for not being willing to take a chance, to open his heart and give himself to someone who deserved love wholeheartedly.

A wave of shame washed over him as he remembered how effortlessly Kat had leapt off the north shore cliff with him, how trustingly she'd clung to his hand. Kat had taken a leap of faith, but he'd been so scared to take a leap into a relationship that he'd pushed her away from him. And as a result he hadn't been there when she needed him most.

He felt for a pulse. It was there, strong, and that was a relief to him. But why wouldn't she wake up?

"I should have been there," he said aloud. "Whatever happened, I should have been there."

And he would have been there if it hadn't been for his stupid pride, his stupid unwillingness to trust someone who trusted him. If he'd lost her forever, it was his fault.

But then, to his utter surprise, she began to move. He felt relief wash over him—she'd been lying so still he'd even worried about a spinal cord injury, but if she could move on her own it was nothing severe. This was confirmed as she arched her back and stretched, lifting her arms over her head languorously. Then she opened her eyes with slow, sleepy blinks, saw him at her side, and smiled.

"Hey, Jack," she said.

"What's wrong?" he said, trying to hide the terror in his voice. "Where are you hurt? Why are you all wet?"

He looked out through the back of the ambulance, his eyes stormy with anger. Why had the paramedics left Kat alone? Why weren't they helping?

"Relax... I'm fine," she said. "I'm learning to surf."

"You're learning to *surf*?" He couldn't hide his confusion. What did surfing have to do with anything?

"I still need a lot of practice. Maybe we can do that together, though? It'll be fun. Did you know that dogs and babies can surf?"

Dogs and...? What?

She wasn't making any sense. He checked her pupils to see if they were dilated. Could she have gotten a head injury?

Your fault, your fault, your fault, the voice in the back of his head intoned.

She put her arms around his neck. "Jack, I'm fine. You know, you were right about my needing a thrill, but that was only half of it. I needed some serenity, too. And you know what? I found it! For the first time in my life I went to the beach and I was actually able to relax."

"That's great," he said distractedly. "But where have you been hurt?"

"I haven't been hurt," she said, less sleepily than before. "Well, I got knocked over by a rogue wave, and that was pretty frightening, but I just relaxed and let myself float back to the surface. I'm getting *a lot* better at relaxing, thanks to you. Well, thanks to you and thanks to all the practice I've been putting in, of course. And thanks to the surfing lessons. Do you want to learn? I could teach you. I feel like I should teach you something after all you've taught me."

He gazed at her, baffled. She could sit up, and she was mobile enough that she could put her arms around his neck. As Jack's fear subsided he began to take in that maybe Kat *hadn't* suffered any serious injury.

"You're really fine?" he said.

"All body parts intact." She smiled. "Not even a scrape or a bruise."

"Then why…?"

"Why am I being hauled into work in an ambulance? There actually was a medical emergency on the beach near my apartment this morning—it just didn't involve me. Well, not as the patient, anyway. There was a child on the beach having an asthma attack, and the family had left his inhaler at the hotel. I swear, we need to give every tourist on this island a firm lecture about leaving important medical devices at their hotels. What good is an inhaler if you don't bring it with you when you go exploring?"

He smoothed her hair. "Sounds like your typical medical emergency. But you still haven't answered the question I'm most interested in: why have you been brought to the hospital in an ambulance?"

"After helping the EMTs out with the child on the beach I hitched a ride with them to work. And I got up so early this morning that I thought I'd take a little nap in the back while they drove." She frowned at the concern in his face. "I must have been sleeping pretty soundly... Jack, you weren't...*worried* about me, were you?"

He was so exasperated with her. "*Worried?* That doesn't cover half of it. Do you have *any* idea how *scared* I was when I saw you lying there?"

She gazed at him soberly. "I'm sorry, Jack. I didn't mean to alarm you. It was careless of me not to think about how it might look to you, me lying here asleep on a gurney. In fact, I've been careless about a lot of things. And I need to tell you something."

"I have something to tell you, too," he said.

"Actually—" she started.

"No, let me go first," he said. "I know you've only been here a short time, but I don't need more time to understand everything I already know I feel about you. I don't ever want to stand in the way of your career. I know that's what makes you happy. So I would never, in a million years, ask anything of you that would be too much for you to give. But someone I trust has told me something I firmly believe: secrets only hurt. So, in the interests of being honest with you, and with myself, I hope you'll let me explain how I feel about you."

She looked as if she was about to say something, but he laid a finger on her lips.

"Kat Murphy," he continued, "from the moment I lay eyes on you I thought you were one of the most obnoxious, bossy, self-assured women I've ever met."

"Wow," said Kat. "Tell me how you *really* feel."

"Hold on," he said. "I'm getting to the important part. Matt was right—I need to tell you. Getting to know you, letting myself get close to you, was one of the best decisions I've ever made. I don't regret any of our time together— not one single minute—and even though it was a short time, it's impacted my life more than any relationship I've ever had. I love you. And I'm saying that without any expectations, not because I want anything from you, but because you deserve to know how I feel and—"

"Jack, I'm staying," she said, as though she couldn't hold it in any longer, and a smile appeared on her face.

"What—? But no!" he said, dismayed. "Why on earth would you do that?"

"Oh, Jack," she said. "Isn't it obvious?"

"No, it isn't!"

She laughed. "No? Okay, I'll explain it, then. I'm in love."

"Kat, you *can't* give up an opportunity like this just for me," he sputtered.

No matter what Matt had said, Jack would *not* be the reason that Kat slowed down in her career. They could do long distance. They could Skype. He could visit Chicago. Hell, he'd *move* to Chicago if he had to.

"My, aren't we arrogant?" she said, but she was smiling gently. "I didn't mean with you. I meant with Hawaii! Although," she said, and the look on her face was tender, "it's not as though you aren't a *very* nice perk as well."

"A nice *perk*?" he said, taking her into his arms. "I suppose I'll have to settle for being a small footnote in your tempestuous love affair with the island."

She laughed, but then grew serious. "Jack.

Let me be clear. I do love it here, but there's an even more important reason that I'm staying."

"And what might that be?"

"Isn't it obvious?" she asked again.

And as she leaned against his chest and put her hands around his neck his heart melted.

"I love you," she said. "I'm happy here, but I'm happiest of all when I'm with you. I don't need to be working at some prestigious hospital to be happy. I can do exactly the kind of work I love right here. In fact, I think I've done some of my *best* work here. Because I'm working right beside someone I love."

He kissed her then—deeply, passionately, trying to put all the things he hadn't been able to say until now into the kiss. When they finally came up for air she rested her head against his chest, and he twined a curl of her hair around his fingers.

"So you're really staying?" he asked, still trying to believe it.

It was so much to take in: that she was here and that she really loved him. Somehow, against all the odds, it seemed as though his dreams really were going to come true.

He'd have to call Matt later, tell him about it…

"I really am," she said. "When I thought about going back to Chicago Grace I didn't feel excited about it. I have to admit that the idea of showing Christopher that he was wrong was appealing. But none of it felt as though it'd be worth what I'd be giving up."

"And what would that be, exactly?"

She grew thoughtful. "A chance to get what I want, rather than what other people expect of me. A chance to be happy." She snuggled closer to him and looked into his eyes. "And a chance at love."

"So, after everything that's happened, you believe in love, do you?"

"Oh, Jack, I do. I really do."

He held her close to him, breathed in the smell of her hair and smiled. "I do too," he said.

He pulled her toward him and was about to kiss her again when she placed a hand on his chest to stop him.

"Wait a minute," she said. "What did you mean earlier, when you said, 'Matt was right'?"

"I guess I haven't had a chance to tell you yet," he said. "I called my brother and we had a long talk about…about everything. I wouldn't say that things are back to normal between the two of us. I don't think they ever can be. But… we're talking again."

"Wow…" Kat said, and he saw that once again her eyes were wet with tears. "That must have been some conversation."

He let out a long, slow breath. "It was. But it's really thanks to you that I was able to have it in the first place."

"Thanks to me? How so?"

"You were the first person besides Matt who I felt I could actually be real with. It reminded me of what it felt like to have someone to rely on. It reminded me that that was something I'd missed."

She smiled shyly. "I think you might have reminded me of that too."

She leaned toward him, her mouth inches from his, and Jack had a sense of *déjà-vu*. He remembered another moment, months ago, when he and Kat had almost kissed in this very ambulance. What had stopped them? What on earth had they been waiting for? Looking at Kat now, he couldn't imagine ever hesitating to kiss her— not even for a second.

They leaned in to kiss, and then, occupied as they were, there was a lengthy silence.

Finally Jack murmured, "Just so you know... there's a surprise farewell party going on for you in the hospital."

"A farewell party? Don't tell me I've been fired again."

"Are you kidding? No, the staff will seize any chance they can get to throw a luau. I'm sure it'll immediately turn into a welcome back party the moment you go in there and share the good news. Should we go and tell everyone now?"

"Maybe not right now," said Kat. "I was actually thinking that this might be a good time for another impulsive decision…"

Kat let her fingers work their way down Jack's chest, opening the buttons on his paramedic's uniform.

"Are you sure about this?" he murmured, even as he began to unbutton her blouse. "You don't want to make a pro-con list first?"

"Hmm, let me think about that…" she said.

She pressed her mouth against his, tasting the salty sweetness of his lips. And as she let the kiss linger, she felt the deep feeling in her gut that was going to guide her from now on— the feeling deep in her body that told her she was home.

That settled it.

She pulled off Jack's shirt.

"Nah," she said. "No lists necessary. Let's be spontaneous."

* * * * *